At River's End

Tales from Nōl'Deron

Lana Axe

AxeLord Publications
ISBN-10: 0692483306
ISBN-13: 978-0692483305

Cover art by Michael Gauss

"When man could endure life no longer, death came and set him free." — *Mark Twain* (Letters from the Earth)

Prologue

Yillmara waded into the river, her eyes filling with tears. Her flowing white gown danced softly on the surface of the cool water. She laid her hands flat above the water and closed her eyes. With her heart, she reached out to the Spirit of the river. *Spirit, hear my plea and grant me my heart's desire. I ask only to conceive a child. For centuries my life mate and I have tried to no avail, and our family is incomplete. Help us, please, and my child and I shall serve you for the rest of our lives.*

Silently she stood and waited for the Spirit to reply. Minutes passed, and she began to lose heart. Perhaps the Spirit did not care for one insignificant elf. What service could she possibly hope to offer such a powerful being? She felt foolish as she stood among the waters. Bowing her head, she wept softly.

As her tears splashed against the top of the water, she realized someone was watching her. Lifting her head, she looked in every direction but saw no one. Looking back down into the water, she noticed a pale blue light swirling just beneath the surface. A sense of peace rushed over her and compelled her to lie back in the water. She rested her head on the water's surface and surrendered herself to the ever-changing current. Sleep overcame her, and she closed her eyes to the world.

When she awoke, she found herself lying on the riverbank. Sitting up, she stretched her delicate neck to the side and turned her face to the sun. Its warmth kissed her cheek and filled her heart with hope. As she looked out over the river, she could see no change. The light she had seen was most likely imagined. The Spirit had not answered her prayer.

She brushed at the sand clinging to her gown and climbed up the bank to her village. As she walked, she realized she was not alone. A second heart was beating within her. Realizing her prayer had indeed been answered, she broke into a run.

"Ryllak!" she cried as she approached the village.

Hearing the excitement in her voice, her life mate rushed to meet her.

"I am with child," she said as tears welled in her eyes. "The Spirit has answered my prayer. We are finally going to have a baby."

Ryllak took his love in his arms and held her tightly. His eyes began tearing as well. He had long ago put the thought of fatherhood from his mind. Now his life would never be the same. "I love you, Yillmara," he said. "This is the best news you could ever give me."

The couple proceeded into the village to spread the good news to their friends. Their immense joy shone readily on their faces. The Spirit had provided them a child, but a price would have to be paid.

Chapter 1

Ulda tapped a heavily jeweled finger against the arm of his mahogany chair as he smirked to himself. It seemed he was always beaming with pride these days. Since taking control of the island of Ral'nassa, he had finally achieved what he always desired—ruling an entire kingdom of his own. Now with so many souls at his disposal, he had the power to take over all of Nōl'Deron. Next on his list was the Kingdom of Na'zora. They had earned his wrath, and he would soon have his revenge.

Rising from his seat, the elf's lean form blotted out the sunlight behind him. His shadow spread before him as his boots tapped against the smooth marble floor of his tower. Servants lowered their eyes as he passed, avoiding the dark eyes of their master.

Standing seven feet in height with an angular face and weathered appearance, Master Ulda looked every bit as calloused and cruel as he had proved himself to be. No one was safe, not even his closest allies. Many innocents had fallen to his wrath in his bid for the throne.

Stepping out onto the balcony, Ulda peered over the edge and looked to the sea. *Soon I will have vengeance*, he thought, his chest burning with anticipation. Looking below, he narrowed his eyes as the servants scattered in all directions. His sudden appearance had unnerved them, and he preferred to keep it that way. They would work harder for a master they feared.

Taking Ral'nassa had been less of a challenge than he had expected. In fact, it had almost been easy once he had the souls necessary to complete the task. Throughout his years in exile, Ulda had perfected the art of soul binding. Though he had dabbled with it for some time, he had only recently come to realize its intricacies. Splicing the soul of a human with that of an animal had been his first step. The process allowed him to create an army of creatures beholden to him. They obeyed his every whim because he controlled their life essence. Holding such power over a being had triggered something in his mind. His lust for power was only beginning.

In time, Ulda learned to place the essence of other Enlightened Elves inside gemstones. To his delight, the power of an elf proved far more potent than that of a human. With this new ability, he crafted more-powerful spells, allowing him to easily subdue his victims. By placing an elven soul inside a gem, he could combine that elf's power with his own, augmenting his magical stores and providing protection against would-be attackers. There were many uses for these souls, and he delighted in studying them and unlocking their every potential.

With everyone aware of his reputation for bloodshed, Ulda knew it would be difficult to win allies. It had taken him years to find the correct formula, but eventually, he managed to concoct a potion that would allow him to preserve the physical appearances of the most beautiful elves of the islands. Capturing and killing them had not been difficult, with the help of his hybrid creations. All the animals needed was a scent, and they would stalk their prey for days if necessary. They never failed to deliver the particular elf Ulda sought. Before extracting their essences, he would administer his new potion, thus preserving the physical beauty of his victims along with their souls. By this method, he could make himself more appealing to those around him, so long as he kept the gem on his person. This undeniable charm had served him well.

Ulda enjoyed decorating himself with an excessive amount of enchanted jewelry. Unfortunately, gems and precious metals were quickly weighing him down. It would require more research before he could bind these things to himself permanently, eliminating the need to constantly wear so much jewelry. Then he could save room on his body to wear only the most powerful souls—the ones that proved too strong to subject to the permanent binding process.

With practice and careful planning, he devised a method of binding the strongest master wizards. Luring them to his tower with his newfound charm, he was able to easily subdue even the most powerful sorcerers. The new process did not involve taking their lives. On the contrary, they lived and lived well as slaves to Ulda's whim. They were his finest soldiers, his elite warriors.

With an army of master wizards at his side, he marched on the island of Ral'nassa, enslaving nearly every elf who lived there. Only those who proved too difficult to bind were killed. He did not have the patience necessary to deal with the opposition, and he had no need for so many souls. The ones who were lost mattered not to him. His sights were set on the Grand Council who ruled the isles.

Upon reaching the Council Tower, Ulda had called out to the sorcerers who held control of Ral'nassa. "I am master of this island now," his voice boomed. "All life here serves me, and you must as well. If you stand against me, you will beg for death before I've finished with you." Given the choice between joining him and dying painfully, most of them had chosen the former. What he had failed to mention was that they would be subjected to the binding process either way. The only difference was that the ones who chose to serve him would become part of his elite force of wizards. The others would be terminated before having their souls extracted. They would live on in eternal torment.

Beaming with pride, he stood upon his balcony and looked down upon his island. The salty breeze from the ocean found its way to his nostrils, and the cry of gulls met his ears. Nature held little beauty for him. Only power mattered.

From his balcony high above, Ulda had a perfect view of any invaders who might come from across the ocean. He feared no one, but he was not so foolish as to allow himself to be caught by surprise. A vast army of soul-bound creatures remained at his beck and call. Looking toward his monsters in their cages, Ulda smiled to himself. His newest creations delighted him so, their beauty unmatched by anything the natural world had to offer.

Splicing the souls of elves with those of the tigers that inhabited these islands had resulted in a beautifully striped quadruped with a sharp, cunning mind. They were the true gems of his animal creations. With the strength and stealth of the majestic cats, combined with the magical power of the elves, he had given birth to the grandest fighting force Ral'nassa had ever seen.

Footsteps sounded from behind him, but Ulda did not look up. No one came into his presence without being summoned, and he was well aware who was approaching.

Prin stepped cautiously through Ulda's throne room, pausing momentarily to determine the whereabouts of his master. Seeing the edges of Ulda's black robe fluttering upon the breeze, Prin proceeded toward the balcony. With his long silver hair pulled tightly back and his bronze skin polished to a shine,

Prin had conformed his appearance to his master's instructions. Anything that appeared unkempt or unclean would anger the master sorcerer.

Prin hadn't been foolish enough to resist becoming part of Ulda's army. In fact, he jumped at the opportunity to ally himself with the great wizard. It allowed him to keep his own will intact and prevented him from becoming enslaved. Most of the island's inhabitants had not been so lucky.

Without turning around, Ulda said, "I need a gift delivered to King Aelryk of Na'zora."

"Of course, Master," Prin replied with a slight bow.

Ulda turned and strode back inside his throne room, not bothering to look upon his servant. A small golden box adorned with intricate filigree lay upon the wide arm of his throne. Flipping open the top, he observed himself in the small piece of reflective metal inside. "See that my old friend receives this without delay," he stated, extending the box toward his servant.

Bowing, Prin grasped the golden box in his hand. "I will, Master," he said.

Ulda began to walk away, but paused a moment and said, "Oh, make sure you don't open it. Only Aelryk may do so." Without warning, he shot a single beam of silver light at the box, sealing it. The magic inside was for the king alone. He did not wish to waste the spell on anyone less worthy. With a smirk, he proceeded up a twisted staircase to his laboratory.

At the center of the circular room sat a large metal table that held a crystalline orb. As he approached, the colors within began to stir. Various shades of red, blue, and yellow faded in and out as the souls of those he had bound remained trapped inside. These had yet to be put to use. Likely they would become the necessary component to splice with some animal and add yet another soldier to Ulda's army. The next step in his research would be to find a way to use one soul to create multiple creatures. Eventually the population of the isle would dwindle, and he would not want to run out of soldiers. Once all Nōl'Deron was under his control, he would have an abundance of souls to work with. For now, he would have to settle with what Ral'nassa had to offer.

Moving to the oval-shaped mirror that hung just above the fireplace, Ulda waved his hand in a single stroke. Before his eyes, the land of Na'zora came into view. His scrying enchantment had worked perfectly on the dwarven-crafted mirror, and it had cost him only a small fortune to obtain. No other craftsmen had the abilities of the dwarves. Unfortunately their souls were useless in the binding process. They contained no magical powers, and trapping them was a waste of a perfectly good gem. Once a dwarf's soul was placed inside, the stone would lose its luster, making it impossible to use it again. Something about the dwarf race prevented them from being used in Ulda's spells. Instead of wasting his time studying them, he decided to focus all his attention on humans and elves.

As he looked upon the people of Na'zora going about their daily lives, he laughed quietly. Soon he would own them all. They would bend to his will even faster than the elves, but first he would have his vengeance upon their king. There would be no glorious death in battle for the aging Aelryk. No, he had earned a far greater punishment.

Thirty years ago, Na'zora joined forces with the only band of Westerling Elves remaining in this world. Their armies combined would not have been enough to stop Ulda and his minions, but the elves brought a weapon unlike any other. A special elf stood among them—a being of remarkable power. Not only did he possess the powers of the First Ones, he also held the power of a water elemental. Only nature's magic could break through Ulda's enchantments, but water alone had not been enough to finish him. Ulda had escaped with his life, but his army lay in ruins.

It had taken these many years to rebuild what he had lost, but he learned much over that time. With his new spells and his perfection of the binding process, he had ensured himself victory in Ral'nassa. His triumph in Na'zora would come next. At the same time, he would turn his attention to the Vale and destroy the elves who once stood against him. Previously he lacked the strength to bind the souls of the First Ones or elementals. That had all changed. After studying carefully the writings of an elf named Telorithan, he had found exactly what he needed. This elf had accomplished both of those feats, and Ulda could now do the same. All it took was the added strength of the wizards he had bound. A simple solution to a difficult problem.

Na'zora's white-stone palace came into view before Ulda's eyes. Nestled along the coast, it gleamed in the sunlight that radiated through a clear blue sky. Waves pounded against the rocky shoreline, finding their way to the soft white sand where Ulda's army had been defeated so many years ago. All was serene—for now.

* * * * *

Prin cradled the golden box delicately against his chest. This was a prize, enchanted by his master, and he would allow no one to do it harm. Though he could not leave the island himself, he would see that it was delivered safely to Na'zora's king. It was necessary to find a human to deliver it, as an elf might fall under suspicion in the kingdom across the sea. There were very few, if any, elves living in that land, and the people had not forgotten their last encounter with his master, whose lineage was that of the Enlightened Elves. Ulda had left a lasting impression, and it was unlikely they would trust any elf bearing a gift to the king. A human who was fully under Ulda's command would do nicely.

After making his way down the seemingly endless spiral staircase, Prin stepped outside the massive tower that served as his master's home. Once, it had been the center of government for the island. Now it was Ulda's base of operations—the place where he crafted and perfected his army of beasts. Prin was delighted to have a room on the seventeenth floor, just across from his master. What better place to serve his needs? No other servant was allowed on the floor while Ulda was present. That privilege was Prin's alone. He served his master's every need, day or night, without complaint. It was an honor to wait upon such a brilliant sorcerer.

Sand crunched loudly beneath the soles of his leather boots as he hurried along the path. Prin knew of several human slaves working in the shipyard who might make a convincing Na'zoran messenger. It would require minimal work on his part to prepare them. With their souls bound to Ulda's whim, they would each gladly serve in whatever role was required of them.

The shipyard was noisy as men shuffled about performing various tasks. They called out to one another in rough tones, and hammers rang out as the master's ships were tended to. Eventually Ulda would possess a mighty fleet—one that would aid him in his plans to take over new lands.

Prin's eye fell on a tall man seated quietly in a corner. In his hand he held a finely chiseled ornament that would soon grace the handrails of Ulda's personal vessel. This man was capable of delicate work, and Prin knew he would fit in nicely among the nobles of Na'zora. For the past few years, Prin had studied the noble families, memorizing their names and locations as well as the source of their wealth. Such information would prove helpful to his master once they landed on Na'zora.

"You there," Prin called, pointing to the man. "Master Ulda requires your services."

The man set the ornament down carefully before approaching Prin. "How may I serve?" he asked in a quiet voice.

Prin held forth the golden box. "I will arrange your transport to Na'zora. Once there, you will deliver this item to King Aelryk. Say you are a servant to Duke Lumbry, who lives in the southlands. Your master sends a gift to please his king."

The man looked down at his shabby clothing. "I am not fit to stand in the presence of a king," he stated regretfully.

"No matter," Prin replied. "I will provide you with new clothing before you leave." Lifting both hands, Prin muttered an incantation. Swirls of yellow light appeared at the sides of the slave's head before dissolving inside his mind. This simple charm spell would correct every flaw in the man's speech and give the illusion that he was a member of the upper class. The spell would last for several weeks, thanks to Prin's own magical skills.

Turning on a heel, Prin proceeded outside to choose which ship could carry the slave to Na'zora the quickest. Ulda's gift must not be delayed.

Chapter 2

From the window in his solar, King Aelryk peered out toward the sea. A ship had recently docked, and he observed with interest as a group of men disembarked. Among them were both humans and Woodland Elves, their difference in height being quite prominent. The short Woodland Elves laughed and gestured, while the taller humans made faces and clapped the elves on their backs. The camaraderie among these sailors was obvious, though this was not the case in the entirety of his kingdom.

Relations had improved between the elves and the Na'zorans, but years ago there had been much bloodshed. For the most part, Aelryk's treaty had kept things under control. Unfortunately, bands of elves had resisted over the years. One of their uprisings had claimed the life of Aelryk's dear friend and loyal companion, Mi'tal. He fought bravely, of course, but he had been unarmed at the time of the attack. Aelryk sent him to talk peace, but the elves had only slaughter in mind. Many good men fell that day.

Turning away from the window, Aelryk pictured the image of his friend's face. How many years had it been? Ten? Twelve? The pain was still fresh. Such a senseless death for a good man. Mi'tal deserved better.

Running his fingers through his gray hair, Aelryk pondered his many years as king. With every act, he strove to improve the lives of those under his care— both human and elf. If he had retaliated against them over his friend's death, there would have been a second war. The ones responsible were never caught, but it won the king some sympathy from the other elven clans. Every elven uprising since then had been met by the combined resistance of both humans and elves. Perhaps Mi'tal's death had accomplished something after all.

With a sigh, Aelryk sat heavily upon his high-back chair. His black satin tunic had become too tight, as well as his woolen leggings. Age had slowed him down and added to his girth, reducing him to the single role of a political leader. Rykon, Aelryk's only son, had taken over the training and supervision of Na'zora's army, leaving Aelryk with far less physical activity and too much time to eat. He could still swing a mighty sword, but battle was best left to younger men. Rykon had done an excellent job as a military leader, commanding both human and elven soldiers. Aelryk took pride as a father, knowing he had taught his son well.

A rapid knock on the door snapped the king back into the moment. Prince Rykon stepped inside, still dressed in his finest burgundy doublet. He was tall and broad-shouldered, with dark hair and eyes—the image of his father in his younger years. The prince was more than old enough to take the throne, and even had a grown son of his own. Aelryk, however, had not seen the need to step aside. Presiding over his kingdom was a lifetime commitment.

"Good morning, Father," Rykon said as he approached. With a slight bow, he took a seat on the opposite side of the king's desk. Placing a rolled bit of parchment on the desk, he said, "We've secured trade agreements with the Sunswept Isles."

"Well done," Aelryk replied with a smile. Rykon excelled at diplomacy, much more so than his father. The prince was well liked among the neighboring kingdoms, but his ability to conduct business with the Enlightened Elves exceeded all expectations. They were an arrogant race, one not given to trusting humans. Few kingdoms ever managed to have their voices heard among them. Now, Na'zora had secured trade with the wealthy islanders, thanks to Prince Rykon.

"The Grand Council's only stipulation was that they would deal with me directly. No other emissary or appointed officer will be allowed to have dialogue with them. They were quite clear on that point."

"That might be difficult after you ascend the throne," Aelryk pointed out.

Rykon waved his hand dismissively. "They will send someone here to stand before me should I ever become too busy to answer their letters." He paused for a moment, then added, "All will be well."

"Will any of their representatives be visiting Na'zora?" Aelryk asked. For a time, there had been talk of establishing a small estate where the elves could stay during business transactions. Naturally they would want to oversee every aspect in fine detail. They were a demanding people.

"I forgot to mention," Rykon said with a grin. "There will be some elves staying awhile in the palace.

They plan to construct new living quarters near the Mage's College—at their own expense."

Aelryk's jaw dropped open in shock. The Enlightened Elves charged a great deal of gold for their services at the College. "Why would they be willing to pay for it themselves?" he wondered. "Normally they would send me a long list of their needs and insist I see to it at once."

"Normally," the prince replied. "This time they want to ensure things are done exactly as they wish. I suppose they hoped to avoid any chance of things not being right the first time." Na'zoran construction was never up to their standards. If they couldn't find something to complain about, they would be forced to admit that humans had done something worthy of their approval. That simply wasn't an option.

"This means they're willing to expand the College with us then," Aelryk said. In years past, Aelryk's father, King Domren, had employed the Enlightened Elves to train human mages for battle. After Aelryk took the throne, he expanded the College to studies of a far greater range. Na'zoran mages now assisted in a variety of activities, including medicine, carpentry, weapons crafting, farming, and even cooking. Scholarships were available to students from all walks of life, as long as they showed a talent for the craft. Though mages still accounted for only a small percentage of Na'zora's population, they were a well-trained and highly respected group.

"The elves are aware that we've been hiring humans to teach magic. They find it alarming." Rykon laughed quietly and shook his head. "They want to send more elven teachers to us at a reduced rate. It's a generosity, or so they say."

Aelryk smirked. "They just can't believe humans could ever be so good at magic."

"They'll always see themselves as superior," Rykon replied. "It's in their blood."

"Nevertheless, you have done what I could not," the king admitted. "I am proud of you, Son. Let's call for some wine and raise a glass to a job well done."

With a gesture of his hand, Rykon summoned the servant who had been standing idly in the corner. "Wine and two goblets," he commanded. With a bow, the servant rushed from the room.

"Your mother will be pleased as well," Aelryk said. "The island jewelers are some of the finest in the world, I hear."

The servant returned bearing a tray containing the wine and a curious golden box.

"What is this?" Rykon asked, wrinkling his brow. He plucked the small item from the tray and turned it over in his hand.

"It is a gift for the king, Your Highness. It was delivered only moments ago." The servant poured the wine and backed away, resuming his at-the-ready stance near the window.

Rykon passed the golden box to his father, who observed it closely. "The decorations are beautiful," the king commented. "Who sent it?"

"The page who gave it to me says it came from Duke Lumbry, Your Majesty," the servant replied.

"He's a man of great wealth," Aelryk stated. "This is a most precious gift." As he pressed his thumb to the latch, the box sprung open, revealing a small piece of reflective glass inside. It appeared to be no more than a worthless shard, and it puzzled the king that such an ornately finished box would contain such a mundane item.

Rykon appeared confused as well. "Could it be an uncut gem?" he wondered. "Perhaps it needs to be shaped and polished."

"I've no idea," the king replied. Aelryk touched his finger to the reflective glass, and a burst of white light immediately encompassed his form. For a moment, his breath was stolen away, and every muscle in his body clenched.

Rykon jumped to his feet. "The king has been attacked!" he shouted.

The servant ran from the room to fetch help, his boots echoing throughout the marble corridor.

Rushing to his father's side, Rykon knelt next to him. "Father," he said, his eyes wide. "Can you hear me?"

Aelryk sat motionless for a moment longer before turning his head slowly to face his son. His dark eyes seemed distant, almost as if he had witnessed some terrible event. Only the sound of a labored breath escaped his lips before he slumped forward, dropping the mirrored shard.

Rykon kicked the item aside, not wanting to touch it himself. Some enchantment was at work here, of that he was certain. The servant returned with a dozen guards and Queen Lisalla, who had been alerted by the commotion.

"What's happened?" she cried as she ran to her husband's side. She placed her hands on each side of his face, and said, "Aelryk, my love, please wake up!"

The king showed no sign of movement. Rykon placed an ear near his father's heart. "He's alive," he declared. "We must get him to his room and call for the healers."

The guards moved in and lifted the king among them, gently carrying their stricken sovereign as he lay motionless in their arms.

"Who could have done this?" Lisalla asked, tears spilling from her eyes.

"The servant said it was Duke Lumbry who sent this gift," Rykon replied, pointing to the golden box. Lisalla reached out for it, but her son stopped her. "You mustn't lay hands on it," he said. "It bears some evil curse."

"We must send riders at once to arrest Duke Lumbry," Lisalla said.

"Leave the matter to me," the prince replied. He would send riders to bring the duke to court for questioning, but at the back of his mind, he knew there was something more at work here. The duke was an elderly man who had stood next to the king in battle many times. The two had been good friends, and Rykon could not imagine either harming the other. Approaching the servant who had delivered the box, he asked, "Who was the man who claimed to serve Duke Lumbry?"

"Just a servant, Your Highness," the young man replied. His face was reddened, and he had obviously been shaken by the event.

"What did he look like? How did he speak?"

"Brown hair," the servant replied. "About my height." Looking at the ground, he could think of nothing else to say. The servant had been unremarkable and no different from anyone else he might encounter working for a nobleman. Feeling embarrassed by his inability to help, the servant could do nothing more than weep. "Will the king recover?" he asked.

"I can't say," Rykon replied. His eyes wandered to the piece of glass laying on the floor. "Summon a Master from the Mage's College," he commanded. If this item was of magical design, a Master wizard would be able to tell. "And see that guards are posted at the door. I don't want anyone coming in or out of this room unless accompanied by myself."

As the servant rushed off to obey, Rykon made his way along the marble corridor to the wide staircase. He ascended slowly, dreading what news he might receive when he reached his father's room. *This is no fitting end for a king*, he thought. *My father must survive.*

Several tapestries adorned the walls along the hallway on the palace's second floor. They depicted various scenes of King Aelryk's life, including his first peace treaty with the Wild Elves, or Woodland Elves, as they had come to be called. Rykon looked at each of them as he passed, each footstep falling heavier than the last. Finally he reached the door and stepped inside.

Lisalla looked up, her eyes full of tears. "He lives, but he is in pain," she said through sobs.

Two attendants stood on either side of the king. One wore the traditional black robe of a physicker, the other wore the white robe of a healing mage. Both men were examining the king.

"What is your diagnosis?" Rykon asked.

"This is of magical design," the man in white said. "I'm certain of it."

"I have never seen such an illness," the physicker admitted. "I will do what I can to treat his symptoms."

"Work together," the prince demanded. "Do whatever is necessary to preserve his life." Rykon approached his father and looked down upon his sleeping form. His eyes were closed, but his face was twisted as if he were in agony. "Do something to ease his pain," he commanded.

As the prince turned away, another change caught his eye. For many years, his father had worn a sapphire ring upon his left forefinger. The stone had been gifted to him by a powerful elf, River of the Vale. He possessed the powers of a water elemental, and he had been of great service to his father in the past. Though the two had not seen each other for many years, King Aelryk considered River among his closest friends.

As Rykon looked closely at the stone, he noticed that its color had changed. Instead of a sparkling ocean blue, it was now a drab gray. Rykon lifted the king's hand, turning the ring for his mother to see. "When did this happen?" he asked.

Dabbing a handkerchief to her eyes, Lisalla said, "It was blue this morning. I'm sure of it."

Rykon briefly remembered seeing the ring when he delivered the trade agreement to his father only an hour ago. The blue stone had shone brightly as always. Could the magic that affected the king's health also have had an effect on this ring? "Is this ring imbued with magical abilities?" he asked. He knew that his father wore it always, but he did not know its significance other than it had been a gift from River.

"He said he could use it to contact River, the Westerling Elf, should he ever need his assistance," the queen replied. "I don't believe your father has ever done so."

"We must use it now," Rykon decided. Perhaps there was a chance the elf would know how to cure the king.

"I'm afraid I don't know how," the queen replied, looking down at her husband.

Rykon wiggled the ring until it came loose from his father's hand. Tucking it safely into his breast pocket, he said, "A representative from the College is on his way. We will figure out how to use it."

Striding to the door, a million thoughts swirled through Rykon's mind. Who was really responsible for this attack? Would River be able to determine it? If the attack left a magical imprint on the ring, perhaps it would be enough information for the elf to discover the truth. There was a much bigger agenda behind this attack, the prince was certain of it. Glancing back at the unconscious form of his father, he clenched his jaw and drew in a deep breath. Whoever had done this would pay.

Chapter 3

Afternoon sunlight filtered its way through the green leaf canopy of the Vale. River and Lenora strolled arm in arm along the bank of the Blue River, enjoying the permanent springtime weather of their forest home. A single robin heralded their passing as it fluttered its wings and bounced from branch to branch. Yellow butterflies flitted about, one landing upon Lenora's shoulder.

Smiling, Lenora held out her hand for the tiny creature to climb aboard. It stepped onto her finger and fanned its wings a few times before heading off into the wild. The fragrance of honeysuckle was thick in the air, and the tiny insect could no longer resist the temptation to sample the nectar.

For nearly ten minutes the couple walked in silence. Throughout their eight-hundred years of marriage, they found it was almost as easy to communicate through silence as it was through speech. As they approached a metal bench wrought with silver leafing, River gestured for his life mate to sit. She obeyed, taking her seat and looking out over the crystalline water. Sunlight danced upon the ripples as the water flowed past, working its way to the sea.

River retrieved a single white flower that had broken loose from the tree above and placed it behind Lenora's ear. Gently he brushed her golden hair as it danced softly upon the wind. He took a seat next to her and rested his head against her shoulder.

Lenora casually rubbed a hand against the skirt of her white dress. "Your daughter was out exploring again," she said. "This time she was an hour from the village before Rogin found her."

River sat up and asked, "When did this happen?"

"While you were meeting with the Elder Council," she replied. Shaking her head, she added, "Alyra has too much adventure in her spirit."

River smiled and looked out into the woods. "What harm is there in a little adventure?"

"She's too young," Lenora stated. "When she's of age, she can venture where she pleases."

"I seem to remember a young elf with golden hair and pale eyes who liked to sneak away to visit the dryads," River said, his tone playful.

"I was older than she is now," Lenora argued, crossing her arms. A smile crept over her face, though she tried to hide it. "It was one of the dryads who told Rogin where to find her."

River laughed. "Then why so much concern? She was safe under the watchful eye of your sisters." Though Lenora herself was not a dryad, she had spent many years of her youth living among them and learning their healing arts. At over eighteen-hundred years of age, she still remained close to her adopted sisters.

"She's so young, River," she said. "I'm not ready for her to strike out on her own."

"No worries there," he replied. "She won't come of age for over a hundred and fifty more years." He turned his attention back to the waters of the Blue River.

"With her always running off, it feels like she's much older," Lenora said with a hint of sadness in her voice.

"Children grow up," River said. "That's what they're supposed to do." The couple had raised seven children in total, with Alyra being the youngest.

"I'd like to have another baby once Alyra comes of age," Lenora said. Looking into her husband's sapphire blue eyes, she added, "Just one more."

Softly he kissed her cheek and smiled. A disturbance at the water's surface interrupted the moment, and both of them turned their attention to the river. A small jet of water sprayed high into the air, a white light surrounding its source at the surface.

"What is that?" Lenora asked, despite already knowing the answer. Someone was trying to communicate with her life mate through magic.

River touched her hand before approaching the riverbank. Removing his blue robe, he laid it on the bench before stepping into the cool water. His long dark hair floated to the surface as he submerged himself, swimming with ease to the disturbance.

Lenora watched as patiently as she could while River conversed with the water. Each day at dawn she waited on the bank while he consulted with the Spirit of the river, but this was different. This was not the Spirit who had called to her husband. Someone else was in need of his help, and she could not guess who it might be. A line of worry crept across her forehead as she watched him swim back toward her.

Stepping out of the water, he said, "There is trouble in Na'zora."

Lenora rose to her feet. "What has happened?"

"Whoever was using the king's ring to communicate was not Aelryk," River replied. "He is the only one who can use it with ease, so the conversation was not clear. I must consult with the Spirit."

Nodding, Lenora said, "I will wait for you at home." She turned and headed up the hill that led back into the village, turning once to see her life mate re-enter the water. As he swam upstream near the waterfall to speak with the Spirit, Lenora's heart pounded in her chest. This could not be a simple matter. In thirty years, no one from Na'zora had attempted to contact the elves. She feared what her husband might be told.

Gliding effortlessly through the water, River made his way to the base of the waterfall and stood near a formation of glistening black rocks. It was on this very spot that his mother had stood centuries earlier, cradling the stillborn body of her infant son in her arms. Here she begged the Spirit to trade her own life for that of her child. Her desire had been granted, and River was imbued with life.

Gazing into the water, River focused his mind to the Spirit. It had guided him throughout his life, and he visited with it each morning at dawn. River could sense its presence as it surrounded him, projecting itself into his mind.

King Aelryk in the kingdom by the sea is in need of my help, River communicated. *Are you aware of trouble in the land of Na'zora?* Thousands of elementals lived in the ocean near Aelryk's kingdom. Surely one of them would have knowledge to share. The Spirit could hear all of their voices.

Your friend is ill, the Spirit said. *He has fallen to evil.*

River closed his eyes and bowed his head. *I must help him,* he replied. *May I go to him?* Only by the Spirit's leave could River travel away from the Vale and the banks of the Blue River. It was a condition of the gift of life that had been bestowed upon him. As a creature of the water, River's magical abilities would wane if he traveled too far from the source of his power.

You may visit your friend, but you cannot help him. His fate is certain.

You mean he will die? River awaited the Spirit's reply, but there was none. He could feel it traveling away from him. His heart sank as he realized why the Spirit had nothing else to say. King Aelryk was doomed, regardless of the path River chose.

Slowly he waded out of the water, returning to the elven village. Lenora stood outside the massive silver tree where they made their home. All elves of the Vale lived inside the trees, using forest magic to create larger homes than a tree could naturally accommodate. They lived as one among the trees, never harming them for their own desires. Instead, the trees assisted, lending their magic to that of the elves. In return, the trees were blessed by the Goddess to grow tall and strong.

Crossing the grassy path to his home, River's feet made no sound against the soft earth below. From the corner of his eye, he caught sight of his son, Rogin, dressed as always in silver armor. Daylight glinted from its intricate design, a runed longsword hanging at his hip. While River and the Spirit protected the Vale with magic, Rogin and his soldiers protected it with steel. River was proud of his son, who had grown to the image of his father, with dark hair and striking blue eyes. Rogin, however, was always quick to act. He did not inherit the gentle nature of his father, who was ever patient and thoughtful.

"There's trouble," Rogin said as he approached his father. "I can see it in your face."

River said nothing but placed a hand on his son's shoulder. Together they made their way to Lenora, who was anxiously awaiting the news they would bring.

Lenora crossed her arms as they approached and slanted her head to the side. "Tell me," she said.

"King Aelryk has taken ill," River said.

"I'll get my things," Lenora replied. In a flash, she turned and disappeared inside her home. Her entire life had been spent in the study of healing arts. Whether through magic or the use of herbs and salves, she could treat hundreds of illnesses. Though the Westerling Elves rarely suffered any type of natural disease, she had kept the skill alive. Not only could the creatures of the forest benefit from her skill, but the trees could as well, though that task was normally left to the dryads. The future was always uncertain, and she insisted on learning as much as she could in case the skill was needed among any race. Any person or creature in need of her care would have it.

River admired his life mate's resolve. Though he knew there was no way she could cure their ailing friend, he would never dissuade her from providing him with comfort. If all she could do was ease his passing, so be it. Turning to Rogin, he said, "Your mother and I will be leaving the Vale for a time."

With a nod, Rogin replied, "I will protect our home in your absence."

Through magic, the Spirit and River kept all those with evil intent away from the Vale. No invader could cross the Blue River, nor could an army march down from the mountains. A dense network of forests protected the only other path into the Vale, and River had set up magical barriers, which he had maintained for centuries. Only those who had been granted leave could enter the Vale. All others were repelled by the strongest elemental magic. No mere elf or human sorcerer could hope to penetrate its defenses.

Rogin and his soldiers frequently patrolled the areas outside the borders. Though he trusted in the magic his father had set in place, it was wise to know what was going on near the borders of their land. Sitting idly and trusting that no one would ever attempt to penetrate the barriers would be a grave error. There were always enemies, though they did not always show their faces.

"The Vale is in good hands," River said, a warm smile upon his lips.

Rogin gave a single nod in reply. Heading toward the council house, he intended to spread the news to the rest of the village.

With three bags full of various medicines and herbs, Lenora felt herself ready to depart. Stepping outside, she announced, "I think I've got everything." She took one last look back at the house, hoping she hadn't forgotten anything.

"Then it's time we were underway," River replied.

Led by Rogin, a small crowd of elves hurried toward the couple to bid them farewell. The oldest member of the Elder Council, Brandor, stepped forward. "I wish you good journey, Lord River," he said, grasping his friend's forearm.

An elf maiden handed River a satchel full of food. "Good journey," she said.

Nodding his thanks, River looked upon the elves of the Vale. Here in this close-knit community, no elf ever stood alone. Neither did anyone suffer in silence. When there was trouble, the Westerling Elves came together in camaraderie, offering whatever help they could manage. Seeing another in distress and doing nothing was not in their nature.

Isandra appeared from among the crowd, making her way to her mother's side. "I'm going with you," she stated.

Lenora placed a hand on her daughter's cheek. "I know," she replied. Her daughter favored her greatly in appearance, but her golden locks were trimmed short, and her eyes were the same sapphire blue of her father. Isandra never wore gowns—her duties as a soldier would not permit it. Not that Isandra would have worn them anyway. She wore her shining silver armor like a badge of honor, her sword never far from her reach.

River looked upon his eldest daughter and said, "There is no danger ahead. The Wildlands have been made safe through King Aelryk's efforts, and I am able to offer some measure of protection for your mother." He grinned slightly. Sometimes his daughter needed reminding that he was, indeed, capable of magic.

"Nevertheless," she said, "there are some questions that can be answered only with steel." She stood proudly and added, "I will accompany you."

With a nod, River gave his permission, not that it was being asked. His daughter was strong willed and sure of herself. She would go and do as she pleased.

Young Alyra approached her parents and hugged them each in turn. Her blue eyes dripped with tears as she asked, "May I come along too?" Though she knew the answer would be no, she could not resist the urge to ask.

Holding his youngest daughter tightly, River said, "You are too young to leave the Vale. We will return soon."

Lenora squeezed her daughter close to her heart and gently tucked a strand of dark hair behind the girl's ear. "All will be well," she reassured her.

Alyra hugged her father once more. Though she loved her mother dearly, she felt a stronger bond with her father. Not only did she share his features, she shared his love of the Vale and all the creatures within it. Together they would sit for hours on the banks of the Blue River, listening to the symphony of birdsong and the rushing of the water.

Stepping away, Alyra pressed her face to her nursemaid's shoulder. Though she had grown tall for her age, she was still quite young. It would be another one-hundred-and-fifty years before she came of age. Her dreams for the future were numerous, and one day, she hoped to travel alongside her father to explore the regions beyond the Vale.

After saying farewell to their kinsmen, the elves headed for the stables where three silver horses awaited them. Rogin had seen that they were made ready, and he carefully tied Lenora's supplies behind her saddle.

"Safe journey," he said to his father. Hugging his mother, he said, "Remember to have a care for yourself while you're caring for others." Lenora had a tendency to overwork herself whenever there were others in need of her services.

"I'll take good care of her," River stated.

Rogin nodded to his father. To Isandra, he said, "Keep an eye on these two."

Isandra let down her guard momentarily and laughed. She clapped her brother on his back and kissed his cheek before mounting her horse. The two shared a close bond, and spent many long hours sparring and honing their battle skills together.

Raising an arm, River projected his mind to the Blue River. Slowly, the water began to lower its depth, allowing the riders to cross with ease. Spurring the horses forward, the trio set out into the wild.

Chapter 4

"Do you think they received your message?" Rykon asked.

"It's hard to be certain, Your Highness," replied Court Mage Ehlir, holding the gemstone close to his eye. "The method of communication is rather complex." Admitting that he had no idea whether his attempts to use the stone could possibly succeed would be unthinkable. A mage's powers were limited, which the prince was aware of, but in this grave matter, every effort must be exhausted. If the prince felt Ehlir incompetent, who knows how he might react in this situation?

"Let's hope it will be enough," the prince said with a sigh. Turning to his mother, he said, "This River owes us no favors, but Father always spoke highly of him. Do you think he will come?"

Queen Lisalla bowed her silver head. "He has to."

"Forgive me, Majesty," Ehlir said, raising a hand. "I'm aware of this elf's magical talents, but has he ever demonstrated an ability to cure the sick? Even if he shows up, there's no guarantee he can cure the king." The elderly man averted his eyes, not wishing to look upon his ailing sovereign.

"I do not know the elf's abilities," Lisalla admitted.

"There must be a reason the stone changed color," Rykon stated. "I believe it to be a sign. Ehlir, make sure every Master at the College has the opportunity to examine the ring. Make every effort to contact the Westerling Elves and convince River to come here. He might be my father's only hope."

With a bow, the gray-haired mage backed away. Though he would carry out the prince's commands, he was certain no mage in Na'zora was more capable than himself.

Lisalla took a seat on the bed next to her husband. Since falling ill, he had not regained consciousness. Tears flowed from her once-sparkling blue eyes, now dulled from the sadness that was plaguing her. The only man she had ever loved was fading, and it burned at the depths of her soul. Squeezing his hand, she whispered, "Don't go."

Rykon stepped away, preferring not to stare at his mother in her distress. Stepping out onto the balcony, he turned his gaze to the sea. The blue stretched on endlessly, the waves rolling as if no change had come to his land. For the ocean, it made no difference whether a king lived or died. The sun would continue to rise, and the tide would still shift with the phases of the moon.

Leaning heavily upon the rail, the prince felt as powerless as a grain of sand. Though mighty among his people, he could be of no help to his own dying father. Only one thought repeated in his mind: River *must* save him.

* * * * *

Darkness began to fade, giving way to the pale light of morning. The travelers awoke from their slumber upon the forest floor. Stretching her arms, Lenora turned her face toward the rising sun. The journey ahead seemed so far. Reaching the king in time might prove impossible, and every minute spent idle was a minute their friend did not have.

Isandra had risen before her parents and was already saddling the horses for the day's ride. Noticing her mother was awake, she said, "Good morning. We're almost ready to get moving." Looking down at her father, she added, "As soon as he's up."

Lenora smiled, gently shaking River's shoulder. His eyes fluttered open, and he sat up drawing in a deep breath.

"I've overslept," he said.

Lenora smiled. "It's time to get moving."

The trio mounted their horses and set out into the deep forests of the Wildlands. It would take at least a fortnight to reach the king, even with River's magic giving speed to the horses. Since Aelryk made peace with the Woodland Elves who dwelt there, the Wildlands had grown far more feral. Massive trees took root, tended by the careful watch of dryads and elven shamans. Humans did not pass this way, neither did they attempt to tame the land for settlements or farms. King Aelryk gave strict orders that the land was not to be disturbed, and none had dared defy the king. The Wildlands had been allowed to flourish, returning to its true state.

The forest was awash in a sea of red leaves that refused to give way in these final days of autumn.

Winter approached with vigor, bringing crystals of frost throughout the land. Only the Vale would remain free of its grasp, thanks to the magic of the elves.

Riding next to her life mate, Lenora commented, "The forest is so quiet here."

Nodding, River replied, "Most of the birds have flown away from the winter's cold. Other creatures are waiting it out by bedding down for the season." His eyes gazed above to the trees, where a leafy nest served as home to a family of squirrels.

"I must have forgotten," Lenora replied with a slight laugh. The years she had spent among the dryads had taken her away from the Vale, but after bonding with her mate, she had rarely left her home. Birds and other creatures were numerous there, having no reason to travel outside their land of plenty. "I suppose it will only become quieter as we approach Na'zora."

"Let's hope so," Isandra cut in. "We might encounter Woodland Elves, and we can't be certain how they will react to us." Ever cautious, Isandra felt the need to protect her kind from any possible threat. "We must remain vigilant."

River smiled at his daughter. "The Young Ones will pose us no problem," he replied. The last Woodland

Elf to lay eyes on River had sensed his true nature. With their return to the old ways, the elves of the Wildlands had reacquainted themselves with the old gods. To them, River was Mistonwey, God of the Rivers. Attacking him would be out of the question, not that they could possibly harm him. Their weapons had no effect against his magic.

A gentle rain fell from above, and River turned his face skyward. His companions enjoyed the weather slightly less, urging their horses to take shelter beneath the largest trees. Without the dense leaf cover they enjoyed in the Vale, the rain easily found its way between the branches, knocking loose most of the remaining foliage.

"I don't suppose you can make the rain stop," Isandra said with a scowl.

River only smiled and continued his easy pace beneath the drops. Reaching into his magical stores, he extended a thin shield of blue light over the heads of his wife and daughter, allowing them to proceed in comfort.

"I don't mind the rain," Lenora said, her lips curling into a soft smile. She had learned to appreciate the rain that fell, knowing full well that it rejuvenated the forest and all who lived within it.

Rain gave way to chilly nights, which grew colder as they approached Na'zora. The travelers barely recognized the land they had traversed more than thirty years earlier. Autumn and winter were alien to these elves, who so rarely ventured from their homeland. Knowing that their destination lay due east of the Vale, they managed to keep their course true despite the lack of roads or trails. The horses were highly intelligent, and easily avoided obstacles without veering off-course.

Days came and went, and finally, River sensed the ocean was only a few more days away. Hundreds of voices called out to him, singing the song of the sea. "It won't be much longer now," he said.

"I wish we could see how the king is faring," Lenora said as she dismounted her horse. "Has there been any indication they're still trying to contact you?"

Though she had asked the same question numerous times over the past two weeks of travel, River was not irritated by it. "None at all," he replied, taking her hand and squeezing it. He could sense her frustration over her inability to help. Until they arrived at the king's bedside, there was nothing she could do. River knew well that his life mate had barely slept during the trip. Her mind was unsettled, and she was impatient to arrive in Na'zora to provide her medical skills to the king.

Isandra busied herself preparing camp for the night. Gathering a small pile of stones, she placed her hand upon them and reached deep into her natural magic. The stones took on a faint blue glow, providing heat without flame. Though Isandra had never been a student of the arcane, she did possess some in-born magic, as did all Westerling Elves. Mainly, she used these skills for wilderness survival when she was patrolling the borders of the Vale. There was little need for her to perform great feats of magic. Such things were better left to creatures of magic like her father.

All three travelers seemed restless this night. They felt so close to their destination, but still not close enough. Luck had provided them with complete safety through the Wildlands. They did not encounter any enemies or wild beasts, nor did they have any problems with the horses or supplies they had brought. For Isandra, it almost seemed that the journey had been too easy. Such things made her anxious.

Rising before sunrise, the group set out early, hoping to reach the Na'zoran border by midday. The trio spoke little, each of them anxiously anticipating their arrival in Aelryk's kingdom.

In her mind, Lenora reviewed all the possible causes of the king's condition. Though she had been doing the same each day since her departure, she reviewed her mental list of herbs that might help her ailing friend to recover. Forcing away any thoughts that her help would come too late, she was determined to find a way to make Aelryk whole again. He was a good man and deserved as much dignity at the end of his life that he had during his life.

Finally, the city of Duana came into view on the horizon. Wooden structures stood tall in the distance, and smoke rose high from the numerous chimneys on the citizens' houses. Winter was in full swing here, and the city's inhabitants were bundled tightly in woolen coats and blankets as they traversed the market district.

Though Woodland Elves were somewhat common in the larger Na'zoran cities, Westerling Elves had almost never been glimpsed. In fact, it was these same elves who had visited thirty years ago, and no others had passed this way since. Many of the humans paused in their comings and goings to observe the strange travelers, who appeared as if from a fairytale. Their faces were ageless, their mannerisms refined, and an aura of peace surrounded them. There was no trace of the rough, untamable nature of the Woodland Elves among these visitors.

Much had changed since their last visit, and many new roads had been constructed. Isandra dismounted her horse and approached a heavy-set man who was loading wood onto a cart. "Excuse me, sir," she said. "We are on our way to the palace district, but I'm afraid I don't know which road to take."

The man stared up at the elf woman, his eyes wide. Believing her to be the most civilized Woodland Elf he had ever laid eyes upon, he stuttered a moment, but managed to say, "This road here, miss." With his thumb, he indicated the second road to the right.

Glancing back at her mother, Isandra asked, "How fares King Aelryk?"

The man bowed his head and clasped his hands together in front of his chest. "He is not well. His attendants fear the worst."

"Thank you," she replied, remounting her horse.

"My pleasure," the man said in a whisper as he watched the travelers ride away.

The roads were kept in fantastic condition. Smooth surfaces and a width suitable for three wagons across allowed Na'zora's citizens to travel with ease throughout the kingdom. Between Duana and the palace district were many new towns and settlements. It seemed that Aelryk had indeed kept his promise to improve the lives of those living under his care.

"We won't make it to the palace district tonight," Isandra said, moving her horse next to her father's. "Shall we find an inn?"

Lenora bowed her head and squeezed her eyes tightly shut. So many miles were behind them, but there were still more to go before she could tend the king.

"We should ride through the night," River replied, noticing his life mate's defeated posture.

Isandra nodded. "Let's at least stop an hour to feed and water the horses."

"Of course," Lenora said, patting her silver horse on the side of its neck. Her own troubles should not affect the noble beast that had so willingly brought her to this place.

Arriving at a small town, the trio dismounted and walked the horses to a nearby trough. Stables stood only paces away, and Isandra set off without a word to collect oats and any other treats she might find.

River wrapped an arm around Lenora's waist. "I know we cannot arrive soon enough," he said. Kissing her forehead, he added, "These days of travel have not been wasted, I assure you."

Wrinkling her brow, she asked, "How do you know? We have no idea what is causing his sickness. Delaying treatment could prove fatal." The final word was barely audible, as she could hardly bring herself to admit it out loud.

"In most cases, yes," River replied, drawing her in closer. "Aelryk is elderly by human standards, but his life force is strong. He knows we are coming." He spoke as much to convince himself as his life mate.

Isandra returned with two stable hands carrying food for the horses. In her arms, she carried a small bundle of sweets to share with her parents. "These will lighten our spirits," she said. Though she was relieved to hear the king still lived, she could sense her mother's anxiety and desired to get her to the palace as quickly as possible.

Once the horses had eaten their fill, the trio was once again ready to ride. River laid a hand on each horse, spreading blue magic over them for a brief moment. Drawing power from the water of the earth, he renewed the horses' vigor, and they pawed at the ground, anxious to finish the final leg of the journey.

With the travelers mounted, they nudged the horses forward. The beasts broke into a run, not slowing for a second until the white stones of Na'zora's palace gleamed in the light of the rising sun.

Chapter 5

Continuing along the path, the road changed from packed dirt to cobblestone. Na'zora's palace district was exquisitely kept, and hundreds of evergreen trees lined the way to the palace. Her heart pounding in her ears, Lenora found little relief in her arrival. What condition would the king be in when she finally stood at his side? The answer was only moments away.

Na'zora's white-stone palace stood tall and proud ahead of the anxious travelers. Catching the scent of the ocean on the breeze, River could not help but smile. Though darkness was looming in the kingdom, the voice of the sea still brought joy to those who took the time to appreciate it.

Nudging her horse, Lenora quickened her pace. Her companions did likewise, hoping to keep up with the elf woman. Riding straight to the palace steps, Lenora hopped from her horse in a single motion, landing softly upon the ground. Three servants hurried down the stairs to meet them.

"Prince Rykon told us to expect you," the bald man called as he rushed toward the elves. The prince had not lost faith that the message had indeed been conveyed, and River would come to his friend's aid. "He's instructed us to bring you straight to the king."

"Go ahead," Isandra said to her parents. "I'll see to the horses."

One of the servants grabbed the reins of Isandra's silver mare. "I'll handle that, my lady," he said. "Please go along with the others."

With a nod, she stepped away from her horse, leaving it in the man's care. The trio followed the bald servant inside the palace, their feet moving at a tireless pace.

Inside the palace was every manner of luxury. Plush red carpeting ran along the hallways and up the central staircase, quieting the steps of those who walked within. Candles burned brightly in gold-colored sconces that lined each wall. Several ornately carved wooden chairs with velvet cushions were situated around the room, encouraging guests to sit in comfort and converse.

Marching up the stairs, the group made their way to the second level, where the royal family's rooms were situated. A wide corridor of white marble stretched out before them. The left wall consisted of a long row of windows, allowing a clear view of the entire palace district. Life-size paintings of Na'zora's past monarchs lined the opposite wall.

Isandra found herself studying the faces of these great men as she walked, and she could not help but wonder why there had never been a queen to rule this kingdom. She shook her head, remembering what she had learned on her last visit to this place: only men were allowed to hold true power in Na'zora. Aelryk had struck her as a just man though. Perhaps he would have changed such a law had he failed to produce a male heir. Perhaps he had changed it regardless. Pushing the question aside, she decided it was best to remain silent for the time being. This was not her homeland, and it was not her place to demand change among these people.

As if he could read her thoughts, River gave his daughter a quizzical look. Raising his eyebrows, his gaze seemed to agree that it was best to keep her thoughts to herself for now. This was no time to make a fuss.

Arriving at the king's chamber, the servant slowly opened the door and bid the guests to enter. With a bow, he said, "If you require anything at all, you need only ask."

Stepping inside, the elves looked upon Queen Lisalla seated at the edge of a large bed with four massive wooden posts. In the years since they last met, the queen's hair had turned to silver, her face adorned with the fine lines of a woman who had lived a happy life, full of smiles and laughter. Time, however, had not affected her kind heart. As regal as ever, the queen's beauty had not diminished.

King Aelryk lay motionless, surrounded by burgundy cushions, his hands folded neatly across his chest. His gray hair had grown thin, and the bony features of his face had become more prominent since the onset of his illness. His breath came in slow, shallow gulps, his expression one of long-term suffering. Clearly, the king was in pain.

Seeing the elves had come, Lisalla rose to greet them. "I hoped you would come," she said, her tears spilling over.

Lenora rushed to her, squeezing her tightly. Pulling a small handkerchief from her pocket, she dabbed the wetness from the queen's face. "I will do what I can," she promised. In a swift motion, she moved to the king's side, setting her satchel of herbs next to the bed. She intended to examine him thoroughly and, with luck, discover the cause of his affliction.

Unable to speak, Lisalla only nodded as she watched Lenora go about her work. Prince Rykon, who had been standing silently in the corner, stepped forward to greet his visitors.

"I'm glad you've come," he stated. "I wasn't sure our message got through."

"Once we became aware of trouble, there was no other choice," River said. "Your father is dear to us, and we would see him restored to health."

Glancing at his father, Rykon forced a smile. Since falling ill, Aelryk had neither spoken nor regained consciousness. His caretakers feared he might never recover, as did his son.

"You've grown quite a bit since our last meeting," River said, attempting to fill the silent moment.

Nodding, Rykon replied, "I should say so." Laying a hand on the elf's shoulder, he added, "It's been far too long. My father holds you and your family in the highest regards. We should have been more inviting over the years."

"Time passes differently in the Vale," River responded. "It's easy to lose one's self and forget about the outside world." His tone was one of regret, his eyes lowered. Seeing how Aelryk and Lisalla had aged, while the elves remained the same, reminded him that humans were mortal. Allowing so many years to pass without visiting one another had been a mistake—one that was too late to correct.

The door flew open, and a tall, elderly man in a black robe stepped inside. Pausing a moment, he stroked his long white beard and observed the elves.

"My father's physicker," Rykon stated. "These are friends of ours from the Vale. Lenora is a skilled healer." He indicated the elf woman who was currently examining the king.

The man nodded, and narrowed his eyes at Lenora. He said nothing but continued to stare as Lenora completed her examination. Finally, she stood and marched straight to the physicker, looking him in the eye.

"There are bite marks all over this man," she stated, pointing toward the king. "What possible reason could there be for this?"

"Leeches, madam," the physicker replied, holding his head high.

"Leeches? Why would you apply leeches to a man in his condition?" Her tone was demanding, a stark contrast from her normal delicate voice.

"They remove the infected blood from a sick patient," the man replied. "I'm surprised a healer would not know of it."

Obviously annoyed, she responded, "Leeches are used to treat swelling in healthier patients. Applying them to a person who is already weak only makes them weaker!"

"This is a standard practice, madam," the physicker replied, waving his hand at her. Her argument had no effect on the man, who was set in his ways and never altered his course of treatment, regardless of diagnosis.

With a sigh of exasperation, Lenora turned away and returned to Aelryk's side. "I don't have time to explain everything that's wrong with your line of thinking," she said.

Stepping forward, the physicker said, "Madam, I—"

"That will do, Physicker," Rykon interrupted. "The Lady Lenora will tend my father awhile. I will send for you when you are needed."

The physicker started to argue but thought better of it. With a bow, he backed away a few steps before exiting.

River moved to his life mate's side, gently placing his hand on her shoulder. The gesture went unacknowledged as she reached inside her bag and pulled out a handful of herbs.

Motioning to the servant near the door, she said, "Take these to the kitchens and ask the cook to boil them for exactly three minutes. Bring the tea back here for the king."

With a bow, the servant hurried away to obey her command.

Lisalla shook her head. "He isn't able to drink," she said. "He hasn't sat up since he fell ill. We've only been able to sprinkle small amounts in his mouth." She nearly choked on the last words. "He's had barely enough to keep him alive." Unable to suppress her emotions, she buried her face in her hands. Rykon hurried to her side, squeezing his mother tightly.

River and Lenora looked at each other, words passing unspoken between them. Laying their hands upon the king's chest, they focused their magic to revive him. A soft blue glow spread across his form, encompassing him for a moment. When the elves removed their hands, the light dissipated, and Aelryk opened his eyes.

Lisalla, who had been holding her breath while the elves performed their magic, rushed to her husband. River squeezed Lenora's hand, leading her a few steps away to give the royal couple some measure of privacy.

Leaning in, Lisalla kissed her husband's lips as her tears splashed upon his face. Reaching up a hand to caress her cheek, Aelryk softly wiped her tears away.

"No need for that, dearest," he said in a whisper. "My time has come."

"No, no," Lisalla repeated, shaking her head.

Aelryk gave a weak nod. "I've been blessed with long life," he said quietly. "It is time, and I am ready."

Lisalla pressed her face against her husband's chest and wept. Gently, he stroked her hair and whispered, "Shhh."

Isandra stood silently near the door, turning her face away from the scene. She could feel a lump rising in her throat but had no intention of reacting further. Death was a part of life, and she was a warrior. It wouldn't have been appropriate for her to break down upon witnessing two lovers say goodbye. This was exactly why she had chosen to live without a mate. Her people did not succumb to illness or age, but they could be killed in battle. No doubt, any mate she chose would be a warrior as she was, and it was a risk she wasn't willing to take.

Aelryk glanced over at River and Lenora. "My old friends," he said. "I owe this moment to you."

The pair approached, their faces shining. "It has been too long," River said. "Forgive our late arrival."

Aelryk managed a weak smile. "Think nothing of it," he replied. "It's good to see you both." Narrowing his eyes, he added, "You haven't aged a day. What it must be like to live so long."

Rykon approached, looking down upon his father, his face stern as if chiseled in stone. "Father," he said, his breath escaping.

Lisalla and the elves backed away, allowing the king to speak with his son and heir. "My son, you will have to lead our people now," he said.

"Father, you mustn't…"

"Listen to me," the king continued. "You must never forget to love your people. Do this, and they will always love you in return."

"I will endeavor always to make you proud," the prince replied.

"I have ever been proud of you, my son," he said, reaching his arms to embrace him.

His eyes wet, Rykon pulled away from him and turned to face the elves. "You brought him back this far, is there nothing else you can do?" Dragging his arm across his eyes, he added, "There must be something you can do."

Lenora spoke softly, "This is a magical illness. It is far too strong for me to break."

"What of you then?" Rykon asked River. "You were supposed to be something special."

"There is a great power at work here," River said, looking down. "It is more powerful than myself."

A servant stepped inside carrying a pot of tea on a tray. All of the room's inhabitants looked at him, and his face reddened at their gaze. Obviously, he had walked in at an inappropriate moment.

Lenora strode toward him. "Thank you," she said, taking the tray. The man bowed and backed quickly out of the room. Lenora carried the tea to the king and poured a small amount in a cup. Tipping it to his lips, she said, "Drink. It will ease your pain."

Aelryk did as he was bid. The tea had a strong lemon flavor with an underlying woody taste that was not at all unpleasant. Instantly, he felt himself begin to relax, the constant ache in his joints completely disappearing. With a slight nod to his nurse, he closed his eyes and lay back on his pillows.

"He needs to rest," Lenora said. "I will stay and tend him."

"I'll stay as well," Lisalla said.

"My Lord River, if you would accompany me," Rykon said.

"Of course," River replied.

The two men exited the room, followed soon after by Isandra. There was no need for her at the king's side, and she did not trust Rykon, who seemed too quick to anger. If he intended harm to her father, she would be there to defend him.

Leading the elves into his solar, he picked up the golden box from his desk. "This item was received only moments before my father fell ill." He held the box up for the elves to observe. "It was claimed that a loyal subject sent it, but the man denied all knowledge of it."

"Do you believe him?" Isandra asked.

"I do," the prince replied. "A thorough investigation has found no affiliation between the duke and any mage. The box is obviously enchanted." Extending it toward his guests, he waited for them to inspect it.

River slowly stretched a hand toward the golden box. Immediately, he sensed a strong magical presence, one that he was loathe to discover. Fighting against the urge to move farther away, River placed his fingers on the box. An image immediately came into his mind. The harsh angular features and dark eyes left no question as to who he was seeing—Master Ulda was behind this.

Grasping the box in his hand, River opened it to reveal the small, reflective bit of glass inside it. Quickly, he slammed it shut, his eyes fixated on the prince.

Isandra rushed to his side. "What is it, Father?" she asked, grasping his arm.

"It is Ulda," he said in a low voice. A sense of dread spread throughout his body, settling deep inside his chest as if a knife were twisting its way to his heart. Turning to face his daughter, he added, "There will be trouble in the Vale."

Chapter 6

Resting her head against her hand, Alyra did her best not to yawn as her tutor, Miss Hilla, prattled on about the history of the Vale. Four other students sat nearby, and they seemed quite interested in what Hilla had to say. Alyra, however, was daydreaming as usual.

Classes were always held outdoors, under the protective shelter of a white wooden gazebo, and too many distractions could be seen as she stared off into the forest. Birds darted here and there, pursuing a variety of insects, and a particularly naughty squirrel repeatedly ran to the center of town to steal nuts that had been gathered by the elves. Alyra pretended she was tiny and could ride upon the back of the squirrel. There were so many adventures she could have with that furry creature as her companion. But when she opened her eyes, she realized that alas, she was still only an elf.

"I'm waiting, Alyra," Miss Hilla said, crossing her arms. Raising her eyebrows at the girl, she pursed her lips tightly and awaited a reply.

Alyra had no idea what Hilla was talking about. In her reverie, she had, without a doubt, missed something. The other students began giggling but quickly covered their mouths when Hilla's eyes darted from one to the others.

"What was the question again?" Alyra asked, hoping she wasn't in too much trouble.

Hilla sighed. "Young lady, I think it's time we had another talk about staying on task. See me after class."

"Yes, ma'am," Alyra said, bowing her head. It seemed she would be receiving the same lecture she listened to nearly every week. Hilla would undoubtedly threaten to speak with her parents, and Lenora would be disappointed once again. No matter how hard Alyra tried, she simply could not make herself interested in her studies. In her heart, she truly believed that she could learn everything she needed to know from her mother and father. Classes were a boring waste of time, and she would much prefer to spend her days exploring the forest.

Alyra managed to pay attention for only a few minutes before her mind drifted away again. Fortunately, the other students stood, the noise of their feet waking her from her dream. She had forgotten that Miss Hilla had planned to take them on a trip to the Archives to supplement the day's history lesson.

Single file, with Alyra at the back, the students followed Hilla down the wooden steps of the gazebo. Sunlight filtered through the treetops, landing upon the young elf girl's nose and brightening her spirits. The air was fresh and clean, and she took in a deep breath as she closed her eyes and continued to walk. It wasn't long before she had wandered from her classmates.

The other students continued on toward the giant silver tree where the Archives were stored. Alyra paused a moment to watch them walk away before turning to face the forest. A group of elves stood near the tree line, so Alyra decided to take a different path and head toward the river instead. Its rushing waters bubbled and sang as they sped along on their journey to the sea, and the sound reached her, bringing a smile to her face. How many times had she sat at the river's edge, her father at her side? It was impossible to count.

His stories of the creatures of the sea and the unique voices of each tiny stream filled her young mind with wonder. If only she could see and hear the things he did.

Though he'd told her she was capable of all his gifts, she didn't believe him. Time and again she had tried to make magic, but even the simplest spells were too complicated. Her mind couldn't concentrate on one subject long enough.

It was only a matter of time, he had repeated again and again. Someday she would learn to focus her energy, and her gift would be revealed. As she grew, Alyra realized those words were probably just a result of a father's pride and his desire to encourage his daughter. Still, she didn't mind him repeating them. She loved him dearly, and every moment they spent together was filled with happiness. With him away, she found herself missing him to the point that it was difficult to sleep. In her lifetime, he had been away only once before, and she hoped never to become accustomed to his absence.

Nearing the river, a strange sensation came over the young elf. Something was wrong—she could sense it. A clap of thunder echoed through the valley, and she broke into a run, descending the hill to the riverbank.

On the surface of the water, she observed jagged silver lines flashing as if lightning were reflected from the sky. Glancing up, Alyra determined that the sky was perfectly clear. The lightning originated in the water.

Cautiously, the young girl moved closer, her breath coming in quick, shallow spurts. All fell silent across the land, as if the world stood still. Another crash rang out, startling the girl. Jumping back a step, she steadied herself and summoned her courage before moving closer to the river's edge.

Instead of the deep-blue hue it normally displayed, the water was turning gray, starting at the edges and moving toward the center. The streaks of lightning disappeared, leaving behind blackened lines that dissolved slowly into the gray water. Alyra's stomach tied itself into a knot. What could have caused such a change? With her father far away, there was no one who was able to converse with the Spirit and find out what had occurred.

Staring for another moment, Alyra looked for any sign that the water was returning to its usual color. After a while, the birds began to sing again, and dragonflies buzzed the water's surface. Except for the color of the water, it was as if nothing had happened. The nagging feeling in the girl's stomach did not relent. Whatever she had witnessed had not been a natural occurrence. She needed to get help.

Turning away from the water, she raced up the hill and back into the elven village. Not bothering to acknowledge anyone, she set her sights to the forest and continued to run. The other elves paid little heed to the child, who was prone to such wild behavior. They had seen nothing of the lightning and were completely unaware of any danger.

Dashing through the trees, Alyra nimbly dodged low limbs and saplings. She paid no heed to her slippers as they parted from her feet, and she ran barefoot through the soft forest grass. Even the thorny bushes that scraped her arms and legs couldn't slow her down. This was no time to tread carefully. She had to find her brother.

Rogin was stationed at the far edge of the forest with two other elves, both of whom were armed with longbows. Platforms had been fashioned in the canopy, giving the elves a bird's-eye view of the borders of the Vale. Here Rogin sat relaxed, unaware of his sister's impending arrival.

Reaching the edge of the forest, Alyra paused and scanned the area. She knew there was a rope ladder nearby, she just didn't know exactly where. The scouts frequently changed their lookout locations. Spotting the rope at last, the girl grabbed a hold and began to climb.

One of the elves heard the commotion beneath and peered down to see the girl on the rope. "Looks like we have company," he said with a smile.

Rogin stood and looked over the edge. "Alyra?" he called down to her. "What are you doing? You're supposed to be in school."

Alyra did not reply until she reached the platform. Not bothering to brush the dirt away from her dress, she said, "There's trouble at the river."

The three men looked at one another, suspecting this was some silly daydream the girl had invented. Rogin's two companions grinned and looked away.

With a sigh, Rogin asked, "What sort of trouble?"

Pursing her lips and crossing her arms, she said, "I'm not joking. I saw lightning on the water's surface. Now it's all gray."

Rogin narrowed his eyes and observed his sister. There was no sign she was making it up, and she was visibly insulted by the insinuation. "I'll come with you and have a look," he replied. "You two stay here and keep watch," he said to his companions.

Alyra climbed down first, followed closely by her brother. They walked through the forest at a quick pace, Alyra leading the way. Constantly glancing back over her shoulder, she made sure her brother was still following.

When they came within sight of the river, Rogin stopped dead in his tracks. Gaping at the gray water, he said, "You must tell me everything you saw."

"I heard thunder and a loud crackling noise," she began. "It sounded a lot like lightning striking a tree. I saw lightning on the water's surface. It went away, leaving behind black lines. The lines faded, and the water turned gray."

"Maybe this has happened because Father is away," Rogin suggested. "He rarely leaves. Perhaps this is some reaction to his absence and nothing more." In the back of his mind, he doubted what he was saying was true. Still, there was no reason to alarm his young sister.

As the pair continued to look out over the water, a large, green-scaled fish swam lazily toward the water's edge. When it reached the shallows, it slowly rotated onto its back, its shimmering belly facing skyward. Within seconds, several other fish followed suit. All of them gasping for air.

"What do we do?" Alyra asked, her eyes pleading.

"We must summon the Elder Council," Rogin replied, not taking his eyes off the river.

"I meant how do we help the fish?"

"I'm not sure that we can," he said. "Mother might have been able to."

"There must be someone else," Alyra begged. Looking back at the helpless creatures as they suffered, she whispered, "Someone has to help."

Looking at his sister, Rogin said, "Listen to me. Don't you dare go near the water." After a silent pause, he asked, "Do you hear me? I'm serious, Alyra."

Alyra nodded slowly as she attempted to fight back her tears. "Could the dryads help?" she asked.

"I don't know," Rogin said. "I can have one of the scouts ask. You are to return home and remain there," he demanded. "No running off into the woods, no getting into trouble." He gave her a stern look, hoping that she would obey him.

Alyra followed her brother back up the hill to their village. As they neared his parents' home, he pointed to the door. Without a word, Alyra went inside. From the window in the sitting room, she had an excellent view of the Blue River. Though it pained her to see what was happening there, she could not resist the urge to look once more.

Tears streamed down her cheeks as she watched the once beautiful river continue to darken. The water became deep gray and had a thickness to it as if it had turned to sludge. Fish continued to surface and die, but no elves came to the banks to assist. Alyra could hear the commotion outside as Rogin summoned the council members to an urgent meeting. Soon, everyone would be inside the council house, discussing what to do next. Alyra knew what she had to do.

Once the coast was clear, she proceeded out the door and hurried down the hill back to the river. A fetid odor nearly made her stomach turn, the smell of death hanging heavily on the breeze. Covering her nose and mouth with her arm for a moment, she took in a few gulps of air before continuing. Her bare feet squished in the mud as she knelt at the edge of the water.

"Poor little thing," she said as she watched a small silver fish join the others in death. Reaching out in an effort to comfort the creature, her fingers brushed against the gray surface of the water. An image flashed in her mind, nearly knocking her off balance.

Steadying herself, she paused only an instant before finding the courage to touch the water again. The face of a man with dark hair and eyes entered her mind. His gaze seemed to penetrate through her, as if he watched her from a distance.

With her mind, she projected, *Who are you? Why have you done this?*

Laughter was the man's only reply, his face twisting into a horrible smile. Alyra continued to watch as the man turned his gaze elsewhere. Wherever he was, a second person had entered the room. Alyra could hear the man's words as plain as day. The second man called the laughing man Master Ulda and asked what service he should perform next.

At the realization of who she was seeing, Alyra removed her hand from the water, and the vision instantly vanished. Swallowing hard, her throat felt dry and swollen. She knew Master Ulda was the man whose army her father had defeated long ago in Na'zora. This couldn't be a coincidence. This man might also be behind the current trouble that took her father and mother away.

There was no time to consider the consequences. Her brother would be angry she had disobeyed him, but she couldn't keep this information to herself. The

Vale and all the people in it were in danger, and her father might be too.

Gathering the tail of her dress in her hand, she ran barefoot toward the council house. Shoving open the door with all her strength, she stepped inside. The loud clang of the door interrupted the men who were talking, and most of the gathered elves turned to face her. Her legs covered in mud and her dress dirty, she only added to the sense of confusion among the assembled elves.

"Rogin," she called. "It's Ulda. I saw him!"

Voices spoke over one another as every elf in the room recognized the name. He was a sorcerer of terrible power, and he had set his sights on their home. Without River's magic to protect them, they would need Rogin's soldiers now more than ever.

Rogin motioned for his sister to come to his side. "How do you know this?"

Bowing her head, she admitted, "I left the house. I touched the water."

Rogin drew in a deep breath and let it out slowly. Swallowing his urge to scold the girl, he said, "Is that when you saw him?"

Alyra nodded. "I saw his face, and he laughed at me. Another man was there and said Ulda's name. It was him; I'm sure of it. I could feel his evil presence in the water."

Rogin knew his next move would be to assemble his troops and increase the number of guards near the border. If Ulda was nearby, there would soon be an attack. Without the ability to speak with the Spirit, Rogin had no way to be sure the magical barrier his father had placed would still be in effect. Once he felt the Vale was fully protected, he would attempt to contact his father.

"Go back home, Alyra," Rogin said. "And this time stay there."

With a nod, she turned and crossed the center of the village before pausing in front of her door. The sky had begun to darken, and the air felt cooler than normal. Whatever Ulda had done, it had affected not only the river but also the Vale itself. Shivering slightly, Alyra opened the door and walked inside. Averting her eyes from the window, she grasped the shutters and closed them tightly. Tears streamed down her cheeks as she tried to block out the mental image of what was occurring only steps away. How could the Vale ever be the same?

Chapter 7

Placing his scrying orb back on its stand, Ulda continued to laugh. The mixture of fear and loathing on the young girl's face brought him immense joy. It let him know that the elves were indeed aware of his actions, and they also knew who was behind the attack on the river. They would fear him, and the only one among them who stood a chance against his powers would now be weakened. River would fade with the death of the Spirit.

Turning to his servant Prin, Ulda said, "Tell me what you know of the Vale."

"Only what I've found in old fairytales, Master," Prin admitted. Months of research had yielded few facts of the mysterious land. "I know it is a land of eternal spring, protected by mountains, forests, and a great river. Mistonwey, the ancient god of rivers, is rumored to dwell there."

With a laugh, Ulda said, "No longer. I have poisoned the river and killed him."

Prin stared at his master in silence. How could such a feat be accomplished? Were the gods not immortal?

Ulda crossed his arms. "No doubt you wish me to explain," he said. "It took years to develop the correct method. In truth, it came to me in a vision."

This intrigued Prin, who asked, "What was the vision, Master?"

"I spent a great deal of time reading the journals of an elf who desperately desired to become a god. That was his first mistake." He grinned at his servant. "Such a thing is not possible. One is what one is born to be. What he should have craved was to have power *over* the gods. That is where true power lies."

Prin felt a shiver go up his spine. It would seem his master was far more powerful than even he had realized.

"As far as I know, no other has accomplished what I have," Ulda continued. "I found nothing in any text on the subject. The method of possessing true power is my own invention."

Prin wrinkled his brow. "The vision, Master?" Ulda had trailed off, leaving his servant to wonder. Steering him back was the only way to get an answer to his question. How could Ulda possibly kill a god?

Ulda exited his laboratory, slowly making his way along the narrow stone corridor, his servant following close behind. Clicking his tongue a few times, Ulda chose his words carefully. "The elf I mentioned before was a fool. He challenged a god; he failed." Chuckling, he added, "The idiot actually thought he had succeeded. At any rate, the gods would not be taken prisoner by him or anyone else. They had special plans for this elf, though he couldn't see it."

Prin still didn't understand, but he continued to follow his master, hoping that he would explain the story. The pair headed down the tower's spiral staircase until they reached the bottom floor. Flinging open the door, Ulda stepped out into the light of the setting sun.

Turning to face his servant, he asked, "Have you ever experienced divine inspiration?"

"No, Master," Prin admitted.

"A pity," Ulda replied, turning away. He continued along the path leading to the rear of his tower. It was a short walk away from the tower where hundreds of metal cages stood in rows. Most of Ulda's animal hybrids dwelt there. Pausing halfway to the pens, Ulda said, "One night I fell asleep after a full day of studying the subject of gods and their power. Upon waking, I noticed the orb had taken on a pale yellow glow. When I looked inside, the answer was there, waiting for me." Spinning around, he marched to the pens, his boots crunching on the gravel below.

Prin was still at a loss. Dare he ask his next question? He couldn't resist. "What did you see?"

Ulda only laughed and laid a hand on his servant's shoulder. "You wouldn't understand," he said, still laughing. "Only a master wizard could fathom it, and even then, only the best among them could perform such magic."

Apparently Prin wouldn't be getting a full answer, but his curiosity still burned inside him. Should he ever have need, such a secret would be worth its weight in gold. Maybe two or three times its weight. Ulda wouldn't live forever, and Prin, who was far younger than his master, would eventually need a new employer. Either that or the money to ensure he would continue to enjoy the life of comfort he had become accustomed to.

"And to perform the magic from such a great distance," Ulda went on. "I am truly a wonder." Holding his head high with pride, he sucked in the scent of his own creations. Looking at the creatures, he commented, "Such beauty."

Prin had no argument with the statement. Inside the cages were a variety of elves and humans who had been hybridized with animals of Ulda's choosing. The master sorcerer did indeed have a flare for creating beautiful creatures. Humans were combined with wolves from the forests, creating a blue-furred hybrid that walked on two legs and possessed massive claws. Tigers and elves had been combined to form a black-striped quadruped with orange fur that glistened in the sunlight. The more-powerful elven sorcerers had been spliced with the increasingly rare wyvern, creating a massive dragonlike creature with the strength of a dragon and the cunning of a sorcerer. These were Ulda's favorites.

Strolling over to a caged wyvern with glistening purple scales, Ulda casually grabbed a mackerel from a bucket nearby. Offering the fish to the reptile, it gobbled it up in a single bite as Ulda stroked the underside of its chin. "Such regal beauty," he repeated as the creature visibly enjoyed the attention it was receiving. All of Ulda's creations loved him, despite their manner of creation. The very life essence of the humans and elves had been drained, as well as that of the creature. Combining their life forces in his laboratory, and adding a few choice ingredients, Ulda was able to craft these marvelous servants by hand.

Previously he had taught his apprentices how to perform his craft as well. It would, theoretically, free him to tend to other tasks if his students could raise his army. Unfortunately those apprentices hadn't survived their encounter with River thirty years ago. But Ulda preferred to look upon it as a blessing. With the apprentices gone, there was no one to duplicate his experiments. Any sorcerers who came after would have to formulate their own theories on how it was done. Ulda wrote nothing down, preferring to keep everything locked away in his mind. He would never be imitated—not now, not ever.

When Ulda had finished admiring his creations, he turned away and stared out over the sea. "Soon I will receive a visit from an old friend," he stated. "Only this time, he won't be much of an opponent."

"You believe River will come here?" Prin asked. The mysterious elemental of the Vale wasn't known to travel often. Prin was made aware of only certain aspects of his master's plan, and he wondered how he would tempt his old rival out of hiding.

With a wicked smile, Ulda replied, "Oh yes, he will come. I have injured him in the worst possible way. I have murdered his god." Placing a hand to his ear, he said, "You can almost hear their voices crying out for vengeance."

Prin looked all around and strained to listen, but he heard nothing. "Hear who, Master?"

"Why, the water elementals, of course," he replied. "They'll all be suffering by now." Ulda's magic had reached deep inside the Vale, penetrating the forces meant to protect it. With River away, the dark magic went undetected, and the Spirit's agony went unnoticed by all who dwelt in the Vale. No other had the ability to stop his magic, not even the girl who had glimpsed his face in the water. What was done was done, and no living man, elf, or any other creature would undo it. The Spirit was dead, murdered by Ulda's own hand.

"That's why you had me send the gift," Prin said, realizing what had occurred. "You knew that River would leave the Vale to help the Na'zoran king."

"Of course I knew that," Ulda said, somewhat insulted. "Really, it took you this long to figure out something so simple?" Shaking his head, he remembered that he had not employed Prin for his brains. He was a loyal servant, as loyal as they come. With a clear insight into the man's thoughts, Ulda knew Prin would never betray him. Doing so would mean instant death. Ulda was in complete control of Prin's essence, though the servant was not aware of it.

"Without River, the Vale will be easy to invade," Prin remarked.

"Indeed it will," Ulda replied, still staring out over the water. He wondered what it must feel like for the thousands of elementals in the ocean. Did they mourn? Did it cause them physical pain? The urge to collect and study them was strong, but he fought it back. This was no time for distractions. He must prepare his army for its first task.

As the sun moved lower in the sky, Ulda made his way to the docks. Normally, he would have sent Prin to check on the shipwright's progress, but his own presence was far more intimidating. Approaching one of the workers, he asked, "Where is the master ship builder?"

Trembling, the man replied, "There, my lord." He pointed to a man standing a short distance away.

Ulda crossed his arms, waiting for the man to act. Seeing that the man had no idea what Ulda wanted, he turned to Prin and raised his eyebrows.

"Fetch him, you dolt!" Prin commanded.

The man took off in a run to speak with the master builder. Both men returned promptly and bowed before Ulda.

"Report," Ulda demanded.

"The ships will be ready in a few days' time, my lord," the master shipwright stated. He stood proud, his head high and chest out. An air of confidence exuded from him, even in the face of his harshest critic.

"Very well," Ulda said. "I must be able to dispatch my soldiers at a moment's notice."

The builder bowed low and backed away.

Without another word, Ulda began the slow march back to his tower with Prin at his side.

"Will you lead the invasion of the Vale personally?" Prin asked, curious as to his master's future plans. It would be glorious to witness the sorcerer in action.

"Sadly, no," Ulda replied. "There is far too much work to be done here. I am on the verge of a breakthrough—one that will guarantee my success. I cannot spare the time."

Prin nodded. He was well aware that his master had been conducting clandestine experiments, and no servants were allowed in his presence while he was working on them. It was a thing unheard of for a great man to wait upon himself, nonetheless, Ulda insisted on fetching his own supplies and performing his research completely alone.

Stepping inside his tower once more, Ulda sighed. There was so much to be done. Tomorrow he would choose which minions would comprise the invasion force. He would also need to test his sorcerers to see who among them held the greatest power. While in the Vale, he needed them to collect the souls of as many Westerling Elves as possible. Ulda himself had not had the opportunity to test his method on them, and they were exceedingly strong. So far he had easily trapped the souls of humans, Enlightened Elves, and Woodland Elves. Beasts of nature were easy, but elves were not. He was confident his method would work on the Westerling Elves, but only the most capable sorcerers would be able to subdue them. It wasn't simply a matter of physical strength. There was mental strength and magical defenses to contend with. Westerling Elves descended from the most ancient line of elves in Nōl'Deron. Capturing their essences would be difficult.

If only Ulda had the time to go personally. How he would love to get his hands on those elves. Too long they had remained hidden in their forest, locked away from the world. They were smug and self-righteous— believing themselves to be the purest race of elves. He would love to show them this was not the case. Unfortunately, his work prohibited it. He must stay behind if he was to finish his experiments in time. The hour of his triumph was near, and he craved it with all his being.

"I require solitude," he said, looking at Prin.

Without a word, the servant left the sorcerer's side. Ulda ascended the stairs once more, following the silent corridor to his laboratory. Countless hours he had spent there, perfecting his craft. His finest achievement was on the horizon, save for a few hours more. With this new ability incorporated among his army, none could defeat it. Glory would be his.

Stretching out in his chair, Ulda stared from a distance at the orb on his table. With a smirk, he wondered if he should take a look at River in Na'zora to see if he had figured out what was going on. Soon River would weaken. Without the Spirit, River's powers would begin to fade, and Ulda would be ready to invade. Keeping an eye on the Vale would be a simple task now, one that would require little effort on his part. There was no more magic to protect it from prying eyes.

Closing his eyes, Ulda leaned his head back and pictured the Blue River as it must look now. Full of venom, crafted by his own hands, the water would appear putrid. The chaos this must be causing in the Vale, especially in River's absence, would be something to behold. He was simply too tired to expend the energy to watch.

Dozing, he imagined his ships loaded for war. Creatures of beauty would climb aboard, ready to do Ulda's bidding. From there they would sail north around the Wrathful Mountains and make their way to the far western shore. A few days' march through the Wildlands would bring them to the Vale, where no Spirit dwelt to protect the elves hidden inside. They would fall easily to his soldiers, and his sorcerers would deliver him a mighty prize. Hundreds of souls, powerful ones, ripe for the taking. They would serve him for all time. Perhaps a few of them could be brought home alive, allowing Ulda to practice on them personally. Smiling to himself, he settled into a deep sleep.

Chapter 8

Despite the efforts of the elves and every physicker and mage in the kingdom, King Aelryk drew his last breath. Lisalla had not left his side since he last spoke, telling her how much he loved her and how grateful he was for the time they had spent together. She wept bitter tears, unable to accept that the love of her life was gone. Her heart was crushed, and she knew she would never recover. Following him in death could not come soon enough.

Cradling the grieving queen in her arms, Lenora did her best to soothe her. "His soul is free now," she said softly. "You will meet again."

Lisalla pressed her face against Lenora's shoulder and wept. After nearly an hour, Lenora gently placed a hand against Lisalla's cheek, spreading white magic throughout her body. Lisalla drifted to sleep, resting her weary mind. After helping the queen to her bed and seeing that she was comfortable, Lenora finally took a moment to check on her own life mate.

River and Isandra waited in the sitting area, neither of them saying much. River's mind raced with worry, wondering what might be happening in the Vale in his absence. He had a nagging feeling that something terrible had already occurred.

Isandra assured him that Rogin was more than capable of protecting their homeland, but it did little to ease his concerns. Isandra, however, was steadfast. Soon they would return home, and all would be well. The Vale was protected both by magic and steel.

Lenora entered the sitting room, a weary smile upon her lips. Sitting next to her life mate, she rested her head on his shoulder.

"How are you holding up?" he asked.

"Better than the queen," she replied with a sigh. "I have helped her to rest, but there is no remedy, magical or otherwise, to take away the pain of such loss."

"Her grief will subside in time," Isandra stated. "It's good that she's resting. She'll be expected at the king's funeral at dawn."

"So soon?" Lenora asked.

"Rykon insisted upon it," River replied. "He says his father has lingered long enough, and it is time he was laid to rest."

"No doubt he is busying himself with the arrangements," Lenora said. "Some of us grieve through tears, others occupy their minds to keep the tears away."

"It's just as well," Isandra stated. "He is a king now. He will be far too busy to mourn long. The kingdom depends on him."

Lenora squeezed her life mate's arm and looked up at him. "What would I do without you?" she asked.

River said nothing but smiled softly and patted her hand. There would come a day when the two of them would part. He had foreseen it. This information he kept to himself, knowing that's how Lenora would want it. Some prophecies were best left unsaid, some people best left in the dark. River had learned to accept his gift of foresight, though it often showed him things he had no desire to see. In all life, there are moments of light and dark.

After a few moments of silence, Isandra said, "We should rest as well."

"Agreed," River said. "I'd like to leave immediately following the funeral."

"I'll see that the horses are made ready," Isandra said, standing. Leaving her parents to themselves, she marched out of the room.

"Is there some urgency?" Lenora asked, her face concerned.

"I cannot say," River replied, shaking his head. "It's only a feeling, but I'm anxious to return home."

The pair stood and headed down the long marble corridor to their bedroom. River's words troubled Lenora, and she found herself feeling anxious as well. Perhaps it was only the distance from the river that was troubling him. At least she hoped that was the case. Sleep would not find her easily this night.

* * * * *

As the sun cast its first soft rays of morning light, the mourners gathered into the palace courtyard. King Aelryk lay upon an intricately chiseled marble slab, dressed in his finest attire. His armor glinted in the pale sunlight, and the edges of his velvet cloak danced gently on the breeze. The king's face was serene in death, appearing as if he only rested before rising once again to lead his people. His eyes were closed, never again to look out over the sea.

All was silent save for the gentle sobs of Na'zora's loving citizens. Aelryk had done all he could to improve the situation of the poor in his kingdom, and no person under his care ever went without food or shelter. He was a king truly loved by his people, and now he was gone. Now they would look to Rykon for guidance.

Queen Lisalla sat at her husband's right hand, her face veiled in black lace. In place of tears, she now felt physical pain throughout her body. There could be no comfort for her. Once her husband was interred, she would have the workers begin constructing her own tomb at his side. In time she would join him in death, and she longed for its eternal embrace. This world no longer held joy.

Rykon approached his mother quietly, kneeling as he reached her side. "Mother, I know your heart is broken," he said. "But Na'zora still has need of a Queen Mother. The people love you, and you can give them so much."

Lisalla barely acknowledged his presence. She turned her face toward him, but stared blankly as if she saw nothing.

Rykon gathered his courage, and did what he had hoped not to do. "As your king, I order you not to give in to despair," he said, his tone severe. "You will travel throughout the kingdom, ensuring that each child who dwells within this land has enough to eat. With your help, our kingdom will thrive."

Slowly brushing back her veil, Lisalla said, "Each child should be offered an education or apprenticeship in addition to a full belly."

Her words were soft, almost a whisper to Rykon's ears, but he smiled upon hearing them. "Of course, Mother," he agreed. "Na'zora will prosper, but I cannot do it alone. I need you." He grasped both her hands in his and squeezed them, his eyes filling with tears.

Dabbing at her nose with a handkerchief, the queen nodded. "You will be a fine king," she said. "Your father would be proud."

Though there were many more tasks to accomplish this day, none could have been more important to the new king. His mother would embrace her new role, and she would have a purpose in life. She would live for the children of Na'zora—to guide them on the path to prosperity.

Rising to look upon the motionless form of his father, he stood silently for a moment. The gathered citizens awaited his words. Finally, he spoke. "People of Na'zora," he began. "Here lies King Aelryk, who brought peace to our land. Under his mighty hand, we have thrived, and we will not forget what he has done for us. We will remember him with love."

The crowd erupted in cries of "All hail King Aelryk!" and "Long live King Rykon!" Red roses were placed at the base of the king's tomb, where he would soon be lowered to his rest. The Woodland Elves in attendance brought wreaths of green to place at the king's feet as symbols of the forests he had restored. Rykon watched with a yearning in his heart, a desire to be as good a man as his father had been.

Hand in hand, Lenora and River stood before King Aelryk one last time. They looked down upon the man who had been their friend, their hearts full of sadness. His death was not natural, and it had come too soon. Trouble lay ahead for both the elves and the Kingdom of Na'zora.

As they stood respectfully before the former sovereign, a voice spoke quietly behind them. "In a million years, I wouldn't have expected to run into you two here. Or anywhere else for that matter."

The elf couple turned to find an old friend, who had come to pay his last respects to the king. Mel, the Woodland Elf who had led Aelryk's men to the Vale many years ago, stood only two steps away. His features appeared youthful, and there was no sign of the last thirty years upon his face. Atop his head was an unkempt mane of sandy hair, and he dressed himself in the animal-skin clothing that was preferred by his people. Over the years, his green eyes had become deeper, their emerald sparkle gleaming brightly.

Lenora immediately embraced the elf, leaning down slightly to match his reduced height. "It's good to see you," she said.

River extended a hand in friendship, and the two men grasped each other's forearms. "How have you been, my friend?" River asked.

"Things couldn't be better," he replied. Glancing at Aelryk, he added, "Except for this, of course. King Aelryk was a good man. He kept all his promises to my people, and he truly had our best interests at heart. Nothing of his father's evil found its way into him. It's a shame to lose him."

"Agreed," Lenora said.

"How long will the two of you be staying?" Mel asked.

"There are three of us," Lenora replied with a smile. "Our daughter Isandra is here as well." Nodding toward the armored elf standing apart from the crowd, she said, "You remember her, don't you?"

"Of course," Mel replied. "She reminds me of our own sword maidens."

"She has chosen the path of the warrior," River said. "Her instinct to protect others is as strong as ever."

"I'm happy to say it's been years since our warriors saw battle," Mel said. "I suppose peace is everlasting in the Vale."

River looked away momentarily. "These are troubling times," he said quietly. "King Aelryk was murdered. Master Ulda has returned seeking vengeance."

A chill ran down Mel's spine. "Ulda?" he replied. "He was responsible for this?"

River nodded.

"Why did he wait so long?" Mel wondered aloud. Shaking his head, he said, "This is only the beginning then."

"I fear you're right," River stated. "King Rykon will surely wish to respond to Ulda's attack."

"You can count on it," Mel said.

In an effort to lighten the mood, Lenora said, "Mel, you must visit us in the Vale. You are always welcome."

"I'd like that very much," Mel replied.

"We plan to depart today," River said. "You're welcome to come along."

Mel didn't need to give it much thought. The Vale was home to the most beautiful forest he had ever seen. "Count me in," he said.

"I must speak with Rykon before we leave," River said.

"I'll gather a few things and meet you at the stables shortly," Mel said before walking away.

"I wish to say goodbye to Lisalla," Lenora said, touching her life mate's hand. Making her way to the grieving queen, she embraced her once more. "Do not dwell too long in your grief," she whispered.

"My son has seen fit to give me a task," Lisalla replied with a half-smile. "He is a good son."

Lenora's heart felt lighter knowing that the former queen would be well looked after by her son. Though he now had the responsibility of an entire kingdom on his shoulders, he would never forget to have a care for his mother. "Be well," Lenora said. "May we meet again soon."

"Farewell, friend," Lisalla replied. "Thank you for tending my husband in his distress. It was your magic that allowed us to say goodbye. I shall always be grateful for that."

Lenora scanned the crowd for River, who had already found his way to Rykon. Maneuvering past the citizens who wished to farewell the fallen king, she slowly trekked to her life mate's side.

It was clear from Rykon's tone that his grief had already turned to anger. "Ulda must pay for this," he said. "My father's murder must not go unpunished."

"Ulda has grown far more powerful than any of us knows," River replied. "We must exercise caution."

"When I find him, I will bring an army to his doorstep. I will have him dragged before me in chains before I remove his head." Rykon's eyes blazed with hatred as he spoke.

"We will work together to find him," River promised. "The ring I gave your father now passes to you. Use it should you need to contact me."

"I will," Rykon replied. "May your journey be a safe one. I appreciate your coming to aid my father. It is a pity you were unable to save him."

Lenora did not take his words personally. She had done her best to treat the king's illness and give him peace in his final hours. Rykon did not blame her for her failure to cure him. He only meant to express his regrets that the illness was beyond her skill to heal. Lenora understood this and reached out to embrace the new king.

"May the blessings of the Forest Goddess be upon the people of Na'zora," she said.

As they parted ways, the wind changed direction, bringing the scent of the ocean inland. The voices of the sea drifted along the wind as well, finding their way to River's ears. They cried out in agony, their torment cutting through him like a sword. It was not the Na'zoran king's death that brought them such grief. A far greater tragedy had unfolded, bringing immense sorrow to all who lived in the sea.

Turning his face to the coast, River said, "There is trouble in the Vale. Ulda's hand has reached our home." His sapphire eyes were wide as he turned to face his life mate.

Swallowing her fear, she said, "We must make haste."

Seeing her parents' worried expressions, Isandra rushed to them. "What is wrong, Father?" she asked, her hand on the hilt of her sword.

"We must leave at once," he said, his face growing pale.

Isandra knew better than to question him. Instead, she rushed along to the stables, her parents following closely behind her. "Are our horses ready?" she called to the stableman.

"They are, my lady," the servant replied with a bow.

Mel sat comfortably upon a pile of hay, waiting for the others to join him. "Finally ready to leave then?" he asked with a grin.

Isandra stared at him only a moment before looking back at her mother, who nodded. "We are," she replied, walking to her horse.

Mounting their horses, the four elves sped off at top speed with Isandra leading the way. It was a long ride to the Vale, and what they would find there was uncertain.

Chapter 9

The frigid air of winter cut the elves' skin as they rode westward, hoping to reach the Vale as quickly as possible. Stopping only once for the sake of the horses, they made it past the borders of Na'zora, finding themselves once again in the Wildlands.

Mel hopped off his horse and placed a hand against the frozen ground. Muttering a low incantation, he reached deep into the magic of the earth. Years as a shaman had enhanced his powers, giving him new abilities to communicate with the forest itself. It did not obey him. Rather, it accepted him as an equal, willingly submitting to his requests. This time, he asked it to create a path free of obstacles, and to guide the elves on their long journey to the Vale.

The ground before him lit with a pale green light, cutting a path through the tangled roots that littered the forest floor. Without causing harm to any living thing, the forest created its own road, a safe passage for the horses to traverse.

Returning to his horse, Mel nodded to Isandra who had been watching with much interest. "That should help us move faster," he declared.

Isandra gave an approving smile. "That's a handy trick. You'll have to teach me." Nudging her horse forward, she led the way along the path Mel had created. Looking over her shoulder, she noticed that the path disappeared as the last horse, her father's, made its way through the clearing. The brambles and roots once again filled in the space that had been cleared, and there was no sign that anyone had passed.

Such magic Isandra had never seen. It would indeed prove useful for the Vale's scouts to know such a spell. They could avoid being tracked by enemies, their footsteps erased before wandering eyes could fall upon them. Unfortunately, none of the Vale's warriors were adept sorcerers. There was a divide among her people, all of whom had innate magical abilities. Some merely placed more effort into their magical studies than others.

Those who chose the path of the warrior spent far more time with a blade or bow, and had no time to hone their magical talents. Instead, they depended upon special runes carved into their weapons to provide magic to their attacks. Combining that with the magic that protected the Vale made it the safest place in all Nōl'Deron. At least, it had been in the past. What she would find upon returning home was worrisome, and she felt it strong in the pit of her stomach.

River became increasingly uncomfortable in the saddle, but he remained silent. Something was terribly wrong, and he had no desire to worry his life mate. There was nothing she could do to ease his pain. The gentle silver horse he rode sensed his discomfort and attempted to step lightly to avoid jostling him. Lagging behind the others at times, it attempted to keep an easy pace while still keeping near the others.

The riders stopped only when necessary to provide some relief to the horses, who ran on and on without complaint. Stopping for some much needed rest, River had visible difficulty dismounting his horse, stumbling and teetering as his feet touched the ground. Isandra, ever vigilant, rushed to his side to offer assistance.

"I'm all right," he said with a smile. "Just tired."

Isandra said nothing but studied his face closely. He had grown pale over these days of travel, and her concern for him was mounting. There was something he wasn't telling her. Not wishing to pry just yet, she dropped the issue and tended to the horses.

Lenora took a seat beside her life mate while Mel built a fire to ward off the winter's chill. River stretched out without saying more than a few words. Falling into a dreamless sleep, he made the most of the opportunity to rest.

Lenora kept her concerns silent, but something obviously wasn't right about her mate's actions. He seemed distant, more than would be expected from someone who was simply tired. She was tired herself, but River could draw energy from the water all around them. His fatigue was brought on by some malice that Lenora was beginning to sense.

With no desire to interrupt his sleep, she allowed him to rest undisturbed. Pushing the thought to the back of her mind, she decided to wait to ask the question burning on her tongue. Did Ulda have something to do with River's lack of energy? She was certain she already knew the answer.

Isandra found it difficult to rest, and Mel was adept at sleeping in the saddle, so the pair sat near the fire and spoke while Lenora drifted off to sleep, her arm draped over her life mate.

"You can sense there's something wrong with him, can't you?" Isandra asked.

Mel hesitated before answering, "Yes." Turning his attention to the glowing pyre, he searched for a new topic. The last thing he wanted was to alarm River's daughter. Mel could sense great evil, and it was growing stronger with each step toward the Vale. Several moments of silence passed before Mel said, "This section of Wildlands was completely destroyed during the war. King Aelryk commissioned my people to restore it."

Isandra took in her surroundings. All was bare, and the ground crunched beneath her boots. "It's hard to judge its regrowth in winter."

Mel shrugged. "You have to listen closely, but you can hear the greenwood that has sprung to life over the years."

Lenora stirred in her sleep, unable to make herself comfortable. Giving up on rest, she stood and made her way to sit next to her daughter. Smiling at Mel, she asked, "How fares the Silver Birch Clan?"

"My people have flourished in the years of peace," Mel replied. "I spent most of the last thirty years learning more about magic and unlocking the secrets of the forest. As a shaman, it is my duty to tend the Forests of Viera to make them habitable for my clan." He paused and grinned. "It's the most beautiful section of forest in all Nōl'Deron, and I'd wager money on that."

"It has been too long since you visited the Vale," Lenora said with a slight laugh.

"Well, it's true Viera does not enjoy a permanent spring, but it weathers the seasons well," Mel countered. "I stand by my words."

"Your people have returned to the old ways, have they not?" Isandra asked. She occasionally heard tales of the Woodland Elves, but none had visited the Vale recently, so everything she knew was only rumor.

"We have, for the most part," he said. "I have done my best to see that the Silver Birch Clan remembers its duty to protect the forest and every creature within it. The old gods have blessed us. I wish I could say the same for all Woodland clans. Too many have strayed from that path."

"That's a shame," Isandra said.

"My clan restored the forests in order to live in them, others did so for gold. They were paid in Na'zoran coins, and they found it easier to trade with the humans using gold rather than furs and items of elven make. I suppose that's their choice, but I couldn't live that way."

"Thinal would be proud of you," Lenora said, her voice sincere. "I have thought of her often over the years." Mel had spoken of her in such detail that Lenora felt as if she had known the ill-fated elf.

At the mention of his fallen mate, Mel felt a lump rise in his throat. It had been her dream to visit the Vale, but fate intervened to take her life before she could lay eyes on its beauty. "I think of her every day," he said in a low whisper. "I see her face in the trees, and I hear her voice on the wind." Looking up at Lenora with tears in his eyes, he added, "I know she sees me, and we shall meet again."

Lenora's eyes filled with tears as well. Nodding, she looked at the fire and remained silent. The pain in Mel's heart found its way to her own, and she mourned the loss of his love. No pain could be worse.

Eventually, each traveler gave in to fatigue and took a short rest. River slept the longest but woke at sunrise before the others. He kissed Lenora lightly on her cheek, and she awoke and smiled up at him.

The horses grazed nearby, enjoying the extended bit of rest. Their bellies were full, and they would have plenty of energy for running until the next stop. Still, they made no sound, waiting patiently for their riders to decide when they would depart.

Isandra awoke and brushed herself off before rising back to her feet. First, she looked around to locate the horses, which had not gone far. Seeing her parents were awake, she decided it was time to move on. Walking over to Mel, who was fast asleep near the fire, she knelt and shook him gently. "We should get moving," she said.

He woke with an audible groan, rolling over onto his back and staring at her, his eyes half-closed. Muttering something inaudible, he groggily sat up and scrambled to his feet. He stumbled a bit at first, but quickly regained his footing. Whether it was morning or midday, Mel hated to be woken. Anyone disturbing his sleep risked serious bodily injury. He forgave Isandra only because he knew how imperative it was that they reach the Vale quickly. However, he had no intention of being jovial. Walking away without saying a word, he went to find his horse.

River rode mostly with his head hung low, saying almost no words as they continued through the forest. Nearly two days passed before the travelers decided to make another stop. As River climbed down from his horse, his legs proved unsteady and nearly gave way from beneath him. Standing was difficult, and he made it only a few steps before plopping himself on the ground.

Concerned, Lenora came to his side and placed a hand against his forehead. "You feel cold," she said.

Patting the back of her hand, he responded, "I'm fine."

Lenora grabbed his hand and looked at it. Small beads of water covered the surface of his skin, and she knew it was not sweat. His body temperature was too low. "What is this?" she asked.

"Just water," he said dismissively.

"I know something is wrong," she said. "Why won't you tell me what it is?"

Staring at her with his sapphire blue eyes, he said, "I don't wish to alarm you is all."

"I'm a healer," she replied. "I can help you." Squeezing his hand, she hoped he would accept her help. Digging in her bag, she searched for some herbs she had brought from home in hopes they would ease her life mate's pain. She sensed no physical illness in him, and no magical one either. Whatever was wrong was a mystery, but she would do anything to help him feel better.

Isandra was already making a fire and readying some water for tea. Lenora passed the herbs to her daughter and said, "Add these to your father's cup." With no further explanation, she remained at her life mate's side.

"We have been companions far too long to start keeping secrets now," she whispered. "Perhaps you don't wish to burden our daughter, but I think I deserve to know what's going on."

Reluctantly, River said, "There is trouble in the Vale. I cannot sense the Spirit, and I do not feel its presence in my dreams. Ordinarily, I would sense it anywhere there is water." He shook his head. "Perhaps I'm unaccustomed to the frozen winter." He didn't truly believe the weather had anything to do with it, but he didn't want Lenora too concerned for him.

Lenora knew he was trying to spare her feelings. Laying a hand against his chest, she spread white magic through his body, attempting to analyze the problem. She sensed nothing. In all their long centuries together, she had never known him to be ill. Trying a second time, she still sensed nothing. It was possible that she simply couldn't read an elemental, but the absence of any diagnosis disturbed her. With any other patient, she could sense their symptoms and often determine the cause. With River, she felt nothing at all.

Taking her hand, River kissed her wrist. "Only an elemental who is also trained in healing could read me," he explained.

Lenora started to protest but then had another idea. "Mel," she called. "Could you come here a moment?"

Mel walked over and stood before the couple. He was not a true elemental, but his deep connection to the earth had given him stronger senses than the average elf. His focus on a single element, and his inborn talents in earth magic meant he might have a better insight into what was ailing River.

"You have training from the dryads, correct?" Lenora asked.

"Yes," he replied. "As do you."

"True, but I'm no shaman," she admitted. "I assume you have skills as a healer?"

"Mostly with growing things," he replied. "Not so much with people." His green eyes drifted to River, knowing what Lenora was about to ask.

Her eyes pleading, she said, "I cannot read him. Can you try? I must know what ails him."

River did not protest, so Mel knelt before him with a quiet sigh. Laying his hands on each side of River's

131

head, Mel closed his eyes and tried to reach inside. In his mind, he saw an image of a river, its surface littered with dead fish. A strange gray mist floated above the water's surface, and the image of a man came into view. He recognized the face immediately.

Jumping back, Mel broke his connection with River. The two locked eyes, and River projected a single message to his friend. Mel understood.

"I can't read him," Mel said. "I'm sorry." He turned and walked back to the fire, taking a seat across from Isandra.

Defeated, Lenora leaned her head against her life mate's shoulder. When the water was ready, Isandra brought them both cups of tea. They did not speak but nodded their appreciation. River appeared distant and tired, and worry was written all over Lenora's face. Isandra had no words that could comfort either of them. If only there were something she could strike with her sword, she would make everything better. For now, she could do nothing.

Over the next several days, the travelers continued the same pattern. They rode until they could go no farther, and then they rested. Doing so shaved a few days from their long journey, and eventually brought them within sight of the Blue River that bordered the Vale.

The travelers sat in stunned silence as their horses approached what had once been a magnificent river of sparkling blue water. Before them was a thick, gray liquid that spilled over onto the banks, killing the grass that had once grown lush and green.

It was more than River's heart could take to see such destruction, confirming the nightmare that had lived in his mind for the past two weeks. Pain shot through his body, forcing his muscles to tense. Slowly he slid from the saddle, his horse unable to prevent his fall. Landing upon the soft earth, he stared momentarily at the sky before slipping into unconsciousness.

Chapter 10

Rykon was crowned only hours after his father's funeral. The ceremony was small, attended only by his advisers. At Rykon's insistence, it was Lisalla who placed the crown upon his head. No woman in Na'zoran history had been given such an honor. It was just one of many changes the new king intended to implement. Women already sat upon the royal council in the neighboring kingdom of Ra'jhou, and Rykon planned to have women serve on his as well. Equality among the sexes was high on his list of priorities, but the more-pressing issue brought on by his father's death had to be dealt with first. There was plenty of time to see to politics later.

Striding with confidence, Rykon sat upon the throne that had so recently been occupied by his father. His advisers stood in silence as the king took his seat. Lifting the jeweled crown from its velvet pillow, Lisalla approached her son with a weak smile. Her heart still ached from her loss, but she had no desire to spoil this moment for her son. Never before had she felt so torn. The pain she felt would likely last the rest of her days, but so would her love for her child.

Holding the crown above her son's head, she declared, "I crown you Rykon, King of Na'zora." Placing the crown upon his head, she backed away and bowed.

Rykon stood as his advisers bowed before him. They echoed a chorus of "Long live the king," completing the brief, private ceremony. Rykon had no need of fanfare. He was king regardless of how many were in attendance. His father's death would be mourned for weeks, and he would not overshadow it for his own vanity. All that mattered now was finding a way to avenge him. Knowing who had caused Aelryk's death, Rykon had no intention of letting the attack go unanswered.

To his advisers he said, "We will assemble in the council chambers. There is much to discuss."

Stepping outside the throne room, he paid no heed to the smiling servants who were observing him. His boots clacked heavily against the marble floor as he walked, making his way to the council chambers. Inside was a long wooden table with a cushioned chair at one end. It had been too short a time since his father had sat there, conducting the affairs of the kingdom. Now Rykon would occupy it, despite his disdain for meetings. Action was better than words, in his opinion, but sometimes it was necessary to discuss things before acting.

Before becoming king, Rykon had often avoided the council. Listening to old men argue and accomplish nothing was pointless. In his old age, Aelryk had become more and more tolerant of his advisers' mixed opinions. He would sit in silence, allowing them to argue a topic to exhaustion. But Rykon could not tolerate their indecisiveness. Soon the new king would replace the majority of these council members with younger faces and new ideas. The kingdom needed a fresh start. Today, however, there was no time for such controversy. These men were knowledgeable, and he would see that they were brief in their words.

The council members filed in behind the king, waiting for him to take his seat before they could take theirs. One of their number was absent, but Rykon was not willing to wait.

"Gentleman," the king began, "there is an urgent matter to be settled. The elven lord River revealed to me that it is, in fact, an old enemy who is responsible for my father's death. Master Ulda has returned seeking vengeance. We must answer his challenge."

"I agree," one councilor said, striking his fist against the table. He was a large man, with a thick red beard. "Our king was attacked, and we must answer in kind. I say we find this Ulda and make him pay."

Several council members echoed their agreement. It would seem none of them were against taking action to avenge the king.

"I'm pleased to have your support," Rykon said, a smile spreading across his face. "I am not one to seek war, but Ulda has struck the first blow. We will find this sorcerer and those who harbor him, and show them no mercy."

The door swung open, allowing Court Mage Ehlir to enter. Under his arm, he carried several parchments as well as a few scrolls. Shuffling across the floor, he said, "Forgive my lateness, Your Majesty. I had a few things to gather before making my way here."

"What have you found?" Rykon asked anxiously. He had tasked the mage with finding information regarding Ulda and his whereabouts.

Spreading the parchments on the table, he pushed them individually toward the councilors and the king. "You'll see here chronicles from the island of Ral'nassa. Ulda took control some time back, murdering all who opposed him, and enslaving many others."

"His army was destroyed when last he marched on us," Rykon said, his expression stern. "How did he manage to take over an island without a standing army to command?"

Pointing to one of the scrolls, Ehlir replied, "He never stopped manufacturing his minions. This chronicle tells all about the takeover." He slid the scroll toward the king. "Not only can this sorcerer bind the essence of a person he has killed, he can control the minds of the living."

"How does he accomplish this?" Rykon asked, his eyes scanning the parchment.

The old mage shook his head. "I know not," he admitted. "His methods are dark, his techniques grotesque. No self-respecting wizard would practice such magic."

"Have you researched this?" the king asked. "Is there a way to undo his magic?"

"As far as I can tell from my research, he manages to bind the soul without murdering the person. I imagine it requires close contact, and an enormous amount of magical talent. There are no writings on the subject because no other wizard has ever done such a thing. Not in recorded history, anyway."

"Why do I find that hard to believe?" Rykon muttered. With the immense power some mages possessed, it was unlikely they would all strive to do good deeds. It was probable that many of them had turned to the dark, hoping to garner even more power. Ulda obviously craved both power and control. "Why did I not hear of Ulda's takeover?"

"Such matters did not concern us," Ehlir replied.

"It seems they do," Rykon countered. Pointing down at the parchment, he said, "This is why my father is dead. We allowed this maniac to roam freely, never bothering to find him after he escaped us before. I will not make the same mistake twice. We must be rid of him at any cost."

The councilors hammered the table with their fists as they sounded their agreement.

"How soon can your battle mages be ready to march on Ral'nassa?" the red-haired councilman asked.

Ehlir shook his head. "None of our mages are trained for battle. They have various specialties, and most of them know some offensive spells."

Rykon looked up from the scroll. "They can fight, though, correct?"

"Nearly all of the mages at the College have that ability," Ehlir explained. "Only the healers do not learn such techniques."

"Good," Rykon replied. "We will set sail for Ral'nassa and knock on this wizard's door. Make sure the mages are prepared. We will be leaving soon."

"Your Majesty," a voice spoke. It was Duke Berl, the youngest member of the council. He rarely spoke, but in this instance, he could not remain silent. "We should not march alone. Seeking an alliance with the Westerling Elves will ensure our victory. They have greater magical abilities than our own mages." Looking at Ehlir, he added, "No offense."

The old man shrugged and remained silent.

"That's an excellent idea," Rykon replied. "With the elves at our side, we have a better chance against Ulda's army." Looking at the ring on his finger, he said, "I am able to contact them through this stone."

Before leaving, River had explained how the stone worked. It was simple magic, really. All Rykon had to do was focus his mind to thoughts of River and the Vale. An image would appear in the stone, and Rykon should be able to speak to it. River would hear the words, no matter how far away he was.

Rykon looked into the grayed stone and tried to clear his mind of all thoughts except River. He could picture the elf's face clearly, and he concentrated hard on the vision. Only a gray swirling mist appeared within the stone. Fearing he was unable to use the gem properly, he slipped the ring off his finger and passed it to Ehlir. "Do you see anything inside the stone?" he asked.

Ehlir peered into the gem and saw nothing. What he felt, however, was far stronger than any vision. Speaking slowly, he said, "Your Majesty, I see nothing, but I feel a powerful evil presence." He laid the ring down on the table. "I would recommend being rid of this object. It is cursed."

Rykon was unnerved by the mage's words. What had happened to River on his journey home? "This ring was in my father's possession for more than thirty years," he declared. "It was not cursed then, and I cannot accept it is cursed now unless some evil has befallen the man who gave it to us." Looking around the room at each of his councilmen, he said, "There is grave trouble in the Vale. We must help our elven neighbors."

"But, Your Majesty," the red-bearded councilman began, "we have troubles of our own. Would it not be wiser to deal with this Ulda first?"

"Doing so would likely help the elves of the Vale as well," another councilor chimed in.

King Rykon breathed heavily. "What say you, Ehlir?"

Scratching the top of his head, Ehlir spoke softly. "Ulda's evil hand has reached far beyond the islands. First us and now the Vale; he intends to destroy us all. Eliminating him immediately might be our only chance for survival."

Turning his eyes downward, Rykon stared at the grayed gem as it lay upon the table. River's sapphire eyes flashed before his vision. In those eyes, Rykon saw something he never expected from such a powerful man—he saw fear. The man who had single-handedly destroyed Ulda's army thirty years earlier now feared him. How was this possible? Convinced that River knew more than he had expressed, Rykon made up his mind. "We will proceed to the Vale with all haste. The elves are in need of our assistance, I'm certain of it. Our chances of defeating Ulda are far better if we have the elves at our side."

None of the councilmen dared argue. The king had made his decision, and it would stand, regardless of what they thought. Some of their expressions grew concerned, but most nodded in support of their king.

Only Ehlir found the words to speak. "What if Ulda is in the Vale when you get there?"

Rising from his seat, the king stood proudly. "Then it will save us a trip across the sea," he replied. "I will see that justice is served upon him. Dismissed." Exiting the room, he snatched the ring from the table and placed it back on his finger. Cursed or no, it was his only link to River and the Westerling Elves. Determined to leave for the Vale immediately, he strode heavily through the hallways. "Summon General Aldryg," he commanded a nearby servant.

With a bow, the servant scampered away to find the general. Rykon continued his march, heading outside the palace, his boots crunching against the gravel beneath him. As he reached the armory, he commanded the soldiers inside, "Make ready to ride. We must leave for the Vale immediately. Summon all the troops in your regiment. I want a hundred men mounted and ready in less than one hour."

The men, who had been relaxing, scrambled to their feet to obey the king's order. His tone commanded urgency, and his men would follow him without question.

Upon hearing the king's voice, a young man rushed to his side. Having only recently been appointed the king's squire, he wasn't entirely sure what his duties were. "How may I serve you, Your Majesty?" he asked, without waiting for the king to address him first. Realizing his mistake, he quickly added, "Forgive me."

Rykon was not upset by the boy's boldness. At any other time, he would have respected him for it. Now, however, the king was in too much of a hurry to speak of it. "Fetch my armor and help me into it," he commanded.

Racing to the next room, the young servant collected each piece of shining plate armor that had been fashioned especially for Rykon. Its combined weight was almost more than the boy could carry, but he summoned all of his strength to avoid appearing incapable of his duties. Breathing heavily under the weight of the armor, he trudged back to the king.

Though the boy had some practice helping soldiers don their armor, he found it difficult to make his fingers do exactly what he needed them to do. No matter how he tried to hide it, his hands trembled as he fussed with the numerous buckles attached to the king's armor.

In his impatience, the king grabbed at the buckles that he could reach and fastened them himself. No harsh words escaped his lips. All that mattered was that the armor was properly fastened, regardless of who fastened it.

Once dressed, Rykon laid a hand on the boy's shoulder and nodded. As the king turned away, the servant let out the breath he had been holding. It felt like he hadn't breathed since he first returned with the armor. Holding his head low, he feared he had failed in his duties. "May I ride with you?" the boy asked boldly.

Rykon turned and smiled. "Not this time," he said. "There is much danger ahead, and I would not risk someone as young as you." With those words, he exited the armory.

General Aldryg approached the king, his stride long and heavy. He was a tall man with a large chest, a thick brown beard covering the lower half of his face. Standing before the king, he bowed.

"I have commanded a hundred soldiers to make ready to move out," Rykon said.

"I'm told we're heading to the Vale," Aldryg replied.

"We are indeed," the king replied. "Ulda may be waiting for us there."

"Will a hundred men be enough?" the general asked.

"I can't spare more," Rykon replied. "If Ulda is not there, he may be planning to attack here. I would have my kingdom protected."

"Of course, Majesty," Aldryg replied.

"You will stay behind," the king said.

Surprised, the general said, "Your Majesty, I am sworn to protect you."

"Yes, but you are the most experienced general among us. I need you in charge of the army while I'm away."

"Your Majesty!" a woman's voice cried.

Looking toward the sound, Rykon spotted his mother, clad in a simple green dress, moving fast across the courtyard. She had the tail of her dress held up, exposing her lower legs. Apparently whatever had motivated her to run had been important enough for her to forget her ladylike manners.

"Mother?" Rykon said as she approached.

"You mustn't go," she said, pleading. "It isn't right."

"We have to go," Rykon explained.

Lisalla shook her head. "Your men can go, but you must stay." Laying a soft hand against her son's face, she said, "Your kingdom needs you here. Send your men, but it isn't right for you to leave in a time of mourning and turmoil. Search your heart. You'll see that I'm right."

Looking into his mother's eyes, Rykon realized that her judgment was correct. Helping the elves was imperative, but his men could see to that. There were many matters at home he had yet to tend to. Nodding, he said, "All right, Mother." Turning to General Aldryg, he said, "You will lead the troops to the Vale. Give them whatever assistance they require. Court Mage Ehlir sensed dark magic upon them, and there's no way to know if our friend River made it home safely. Be vigilant in the Wildlands."

"Of course, Your Majesty," Aldryg replied. "I will do as you command."

"Also," Rykon added, "it is important that we create an alliance with the elves. I intend to attack Ulda at his lair on Ral'nassa, assuming he is still there. I would have the elves march with me."

"Understood, Majesty," the general stated.

"Safe travels," the king said. He waited a moment to watch his general walk away. Soldiers were already filing into the courtyard as they prepared to head out. Taking his mother by the arm, he escorted her back inside the palace. Looking down at the ring once more, he hoped it would show a different picture soon—one that was far less ominous.

Chapter 11

Swinging her leg over her horse's neck, Isandra hopped down and rushed to her father's aid. He lay unmoving on the ground as she knelt beside him and lifted his head. "Father!" she called, but he did not reply.

Lenora could barely move, her body numb all over, but somehow she managed to get to her life mate. She squeezed his hand and spoke in a soft voice. "Hold on," she repeated over and over.

Mel waved his arms to the scout who was standing on the far bank of the river. Recognizing Isandra's horse, the elf immediately kicked his raft away from the bank and floated over to lend a hand.

Isandra and Mel lifted River and placed him gently upon the raft. He stirred only slightly, but he did not open his eyes or speak.

"Don't touch the water," the scout said, extending a hand to Lenora. Helping her take a seat on the raft, he immediately paddled back toward the Vale.

Lenora propped River's head on her lap as they slowly crossed over the water. Looking down, her vision could not penetrate its depths. What was once crystal clear to the bottom was now an opaque gray liquid. A putrid smell emitted from the river, and her eyes fell upon the numerous dead fish floating near the edges. *Why?* She could not understand why Ulda had done this, but she knew without a doubt that he was behind it. No other could be so cruel.

When they reached the shore, Isandra took her father's shoulders and Mel took his feet, while the elf scout supported his back. The trio, followed by Lenora, proceeded up the hill and through the village. A crowd of onlookers gathered to watch, many of them clasping their hands over their mouths. River's condition was even more concerning than the changes in the Blue River.

Hearing the commotion outside, Alyra rushed to the front door. Through the window, she saw her mother and breathed a sigh of relief. Finally, her parents had returned. When she opened the door and saw her father, she shrieked, "What happened?"

"Your father isn't well," Lenora replied, gently laying a hand on her daughter's shoulder. "Take him upstairs," she said to Isandra.

"What's wrong with him?" Alyra asked, tears spilling from her eyes.

Lenora reached for her daughter and squeezed her tightly to her side as she ascended the steps. "It's Ulda's dark magic," she said. "We must make your father comfortable and allow him to rest." Kissing her daughter's forehead, she added, "You can fetch some herbs for me."

Alyra nodded without hearing what her mother had said. Her mind was focused on her father as the three elves carried him inside his room and placed him gently upon his bed. Lenora immediately went to his side, laying her hands on each side of his head. Spreading white magic over his body, she searched for the cause of his unconscious state.

Alyra stood frozen in the doorway, staring at her parents. She did not see Isandra approaching her, and she jumped at the sound of her sister's voice.

"Mother will see to him," Isandra said, attempting to reassure the young girl. "There is no better healer in the Vale." Kneeling next to her sister, she mussed her hair and smiled. Alyra paid her no heed. Frowning, Isandra said, "Come with me for a walk."

Alyra shook her head. "I want to stay here," she insisted. "Please don't make me go." Tears slid down her cheeks before splashing to the floor.

"All right," Isandra replied softly. Taking Alyra by the hand, she led the girl to her mother's cushioned chair. "Stay quiet and do whatever mother tells you," she said. "I'm going to find Rogin."

Alyra nodded, her eyes still locked on her parents. Finally, Lenora pulled her hands away from her life mate. Alyra sat forward, scooting to the edge of her seat. Mel stood silently to the side, awaiting the diagnosis.

"He's exhausted," Lenora said. Turning to Mel, she added, "The best I can tell, he is depleted of magic." Though her heart was pounding and her head felt like it might explode, she managed to keep her composure.

"We should let him rest then," Mel said. "After he's had some time, we can share magic with him if he needs it."

Under normal circumstances, elementals could not deplete their own magical supply. They had a special ability to absorb magic from the element they represent. River, despite being only partly an elemental, had a massive store of magic. Lenora had never known him to exhaust his supply.

Mel was certain River's condition was directly related to the curse Ulda had laid upon the Blue River. Luckily, there were many elves around with magical abilities who could share power with the ailing elf. In theory, he should be able to recover, assuming that was his only problem.

"I can craft medicine to help him recover faster," Lenora said quietly. "Alyra, can you fetch some items for me from my study?"

Alyra jumped to her feet, eager to help her mother. "Of course," she said.

Lenora moved to her desk to find a scrap of parchment. Quickly, she listed the items she would need and passed it to her daughter. "Fetch these quickly," she said. "I'll stay with him."

Alyra scampered away, her footsteps echoing through the hallway as she ran farther up the stairs.

Mel stepped forward and said, "You should rest as well, Lenora. We don't want you falling ill."

Nodding, Lenora replied, "Once I've given him the elixir, I'll rest beside him in case he wakes."

It was only a few moments before Alyra returned, carrying every item her mother had requested. Her little arms were stuffed full, and Mel rushed to help her as she appeared in the doorway.

Finding some of the items to be quite heavy for a young girl, Mel asked, "You can carry all this?"

She nodded quickly, not paying attention to the grin on his face. Helping her mother to spread the items out on the table, she asked, "Can I help you measure the ingredients?"

With a slight smile, Lenora responded, "Of course."

Once the draught was ready, Lenora placed it in a dropper and allowed Alyra to open her father's mouth. "Tilt his head back," she told the girl. Dropping the medicine slowly down his throat, she felt content that it would work. All he needed was time to recover from his depletion, and he would be well enough to speak and help her figure out what to do next. Not having his input was alien to her. The two had always worked together, and she felt lost without him.

Curling up on the bed next to her life mate, Lenora reached her arm across his chest and hugged him. Snuggled next to him, she quickly drifted off to sleep.

Alyra chewed on her bottom lip. Watching the pair sleep was almost as nerve racking as seeing her father ill. She searched her mind, trying to find a way to help while her parents slept.

"Why don't you come outside with me?" Mel asked. "It's better than standing around waiting."

Glancing between her parents and Mel, Alyra decided. "Okay," she said, following Mel down the stairs.

They stepped outside into the chilly air. "Why is it so cold here?" Mel wondered.

"It's been like that since the river turned gray," Alyra explained.

"Ah," he replied. "All part of Ulda's plan, I guess." Spotting Isandra and Rogin only steps away, he crossed the dying grass to speak with them.

"This is Mel," Isandra said.

"I remember," Rogin replied with a smile. "Welcome. I wish your visit was under better circumstances."

"I didn't realize what was going on here, or I might have stayed home," Mel said casually. It was true. With trouble brewing in the Vale, his own home might also be in jeopardy. It was his clan who had stood against Ulda when no other Woodland Elves had even considered it.

"So far our scouts haven't spotted anything out of the ordinary," Rogin stated, "except for the river and the strange weather. There have been no strange creatures and no attacks upon any of the creatures of the forest. No one has attempted to enter the Vale."

"Your magical barriers are gone," Mel informed them.

Isandra and Rogin exchanged worried glances.

"How do you know?" Alyra asked, voicing what her siblings could not.

"I could sense the magic the last time I was here," he explained. "It can't be seen, but it can be felt if you are attuned to its frequency."

"Is that part of being a shaman?" the girl wondered.

"I guess so," Mel replied. "I never really understood where my powers came from, but when they manifested themselves, they were strong." Studying Alyra's features, he said, "I sense a lot in you."

"I can't do magic," Alyra replied, looking down at her feet. "Not anything important anyway."

"You will," Mel replied.

Alyra had heard that before, so she didn't pay any special attention to Mel's words.

"You are a master of earth magic," Isandra said to Mel. "Would you scout the perimeter with us and tell us if you sense anything?"

"You think your brother's men might have missed something?" Mel joked with a grin. "I guess I can make myself useful."

The trio started to walk away and leave Alyra behind. "Can I come?" she asked.

"You should stay in town," Rogin replied. "The forest isn't safe."

"You just said you hadn't seen anything out of the ordinary," the girl replied, crossing her arms.

"She's got you there," Mel said. With a wave of his hand, he invited Alyra to join them.

* * * * *

River awoke still feeling exhausted. Managing a weak smile, he placed his hand on his life mate's head as she slept next to him. She awoke as he stroked her golden tresses.

Sitting up, she cried, "River!" Wrapping her arms around him, she buried her face against his chest. "I was so worried," she said.

"I'm better now, thanks to you," he said, his tone even and quiet. Though he was still not at full strength, he felt well enough to speak. "I need to speak to Mel," he said.

Nodding, Lenora replied, "I'll find him for you." Kissing him gently, she rose from the bed and made her way down the stairs. Luckily, Mel was not far. After scouting the forest, he and Lenora's children had returned to wait outside her home. "He is awake," she announced, "and he would like to speak with you, Mel."

Alyra ran to her mother and squeezed her tightly before heading inside and running up the stairs. Entering her parents' room, she ran to her father and jumped onto the bed. He smiled upon seeing her and wrapped his arms around her, squeezing her as tightly as he could.

"It's good to see you," he said.

"You scared me," she scolded. "What's wrong with you?"

Shaking his head, he replied, "Just tired is all."

Lenora entered along with Mel, Isandra, and Rogin. Alyra climbed off of the bed and moved to the far side of the room, hoping she wouldn't be asked to leave.

"Do you sense anything?" River asked Mel.

"I don't sense any presence if that's what you're asking," he replied. Without bothering to sugarcoat it, he added, "I see Ulda's face when I look toward the river."

River closed his eyes and nodded slowly.

Rogin stepped forward and declared, "My men are ready to march. Let us be rid of this threat once and for all."

River held up a hand to silence him. "You are needed in the Vale now more than ever. You must remain here to protect it. Isandra as well."

Exhaling loudly, Rogin stepped back and stood next to his sister, his hand resting on the hilt of his sword. Staring at his father, he hoped to hear an explanation.

"Ulda has laid a curse on the land," River stated. "He has poisoned the river and destroyed the Spirit. By what means I do not know."

Lenora gasped, covering her mouth with her hands. What did this mean for her life mate? The Spirit had granted him life. With the Spirit gone, how would

River continue? She tried hard to swallow the questions, but a lump rose in her throat, preventing it. "What will this mean for us?" she asked, tears streaming down her cheeks.

"It means we must be strong," he replied. "Ulda threatens not only the Vale but all the world." He waved at Mel to come closer, and the elf obeyed. "Ulda has grown in strength since our last meeting. I need your help."

"Anything," Mel replied.

"The water is poisonous, and no elf here can touch it, except for you and me," River said. His eyes darted briefly to Alyra, who looked down at her feet.

Mel didn't understand. "Why wouldn't it be poisonous to me?"

"The earth protects you," River explained. "I need you to bring one of the fish to me."

"They're all dead."

"I'm aware of that," River said, frowning. "I wish I had been here to protect them." After a moment, he repeated, "I need you to bring one of them to me."

With a nod, Mel headed down to the banks of the river where dozens of dead fish were floating, their cloudy eyes staring blankly at the sky. Nearly retching from the stench, he reached in and grabbed a small fish, which quickly fell apart in his grasp. "This had better be important," he muttered under his breath. Grabbing another fish, he was relieved to see it held together. Holding it by the tail, he brought it inside and presented it before River. "One disgusting, stinking fish," he said.

River pressed his hands against the fish's side and closed his eyes. He experienced the last moments of the fish's life as it gasped for air at the surface. Concentrating harder, he moved back in time to the moment the river had been poisoned. Ulda and the Spirit had fought, with Ulda keeping himself at a distance. Through his orb, he projected his magic, attempting to bind the Spirit and extract its essence. Ulda had failed, but the Spirit was destroyed. The magical strength necessary to accomplish this feat was unfathomable. How had Ulda gained such power?

Opening his eyes, River seemed more tired than before. Using magic to read the fish's memories had taken more effort than he expected. After taking a few deep breaths, he asked, "Rogin, will you take this poor creature away?"

Rogin obeyed, taking the fish from his father. He carried it to the doorway but paused, hoping to avoid missing any important words his father might say.

"We are lucky," River said. "Ulda was not able to bind the Spirit. If he had, he would be unstoppable. As it is, he is already stronger than both of us."

"And where does the luck come in?" Mel asked. He wasn't exactly feeling very lucky.

"The luck is that, in his failure, he left himself vulnerable," River replied, resting his head back on his pillow. "There is a way to defeat him."

Mel waited a moment and glanced back over his shoulder. It seemed that River had fallen asleep. Speaking a little louder, he asked, "And how is that?"

Without opening his eyes, River replied, "We must unite the elements."

Chapter 12

Standing at the coastline, his heels digging into the wet sand, Ulda watched with fatherly pride as his creations boarded the ship that would carry them to the Vale. Among them were three sorcerers, hand-picked by the master wizard. They would ride upon wyverns and lead the other creatures in an attack on the Westerling Elves. These sorcerers were among the most skilled, and Ulda felt certain they would succeed in binding elven souls to bring to him. In addition, he ordered them to bring back living prisoners so he could bind them himself. That would ensure that the process was done properly, and fewer souls would go to waste.

The invasion wasn't solely about gaining control of the Vale. Rather, it was a method of binding the strongest elven essences in all Nōl'Deron. Their power would grant Ulda the boost he needed to continue his secret research. Soon he would perfect the mechanism that would render his army unstoppable.

Sucking in a deep gulp of air, Ulda smiled at the wind. The sails of the ship billowed as if the ship were eager to get underway. It was a perfect morning to set sail. With the wind in their favor, the ships would travel faster, and Ulda would not have to wait too long to witness the destruction of the Vale. Though he would not be there in person, he would witness every moment of battle through his scrying orb. It would be a welcome break from his research.

Counting each creature as they passed, Ulda made certain that his orders had been followed to the letter. Forty wolfbeasts, forty man-size spiders, forty tigers, and two-hundred soul-bound elven foot soldiers. In addition to the elite sorcerers with their wyverns, Ulda expected his army to easily break the lines of the Westerling Elves. Their numbers were waning, as the elders continued to cross over faster than the younger elves could give birth. So few were left in the world that if Ulda didn't act in the next century or two, there might be none of the race left to collect. It would be a pity for such a species to go to waste. Ulda had great plans for them.

The ship's captain made his way down the gangplank after the last of the soldiers had boarded. Bowing low, he said, "We are ready to disembark, Master." Avoiding Ulda's gaze, he stared down at his boots.

"I will monitor your progress," Ulda responded. "I expect the ship to return in one piece with as many prisoners as it can hold."

The captain nodded and backed away. Never feeling safe in Ulda's presence, he hurried back to the deck of his ship, where he was ever at home. The farther he sailed from Ulda, the safer he would feel, despite heading out to battle. On the sea, he knew what to expect. Standing next to the sorcerer, he could never shake the feeling he was about to be set ablaze. Focusing on his duties to the ship kept him out of trouble. As long as the ship remained in good condition, Ulda had no reason to be angry with the captain.

Ulda stayed to observe as the crew pulled up the anchor and set sail. It would be days before it arrived in the Vale, and Ulda would have to live with the anxiety. How thrilling it was for him to know that soon he would possess so many powerful souls. The descendants of the Ancient Ones were only slightly less valuable than elementals. Nearly salivating at the thought, he could not stop himself from smiling.

With a wave of his hand, he bid Prin to follow as he made his way across the sand to return to his tower. "We must check on things in Na'zora," he said. "I've neglected them for far too long." His attack on the Spirit of the river had taken more time and effort than anticipated. That coupled with readying his forces for their journey, he had not taken the time to see how the kingdom had reacted to Aelryk's death.

Climbing the spiral steps, he entered his laboratory and barked at the servants inside as they attempted to clean away the dust. "Out!" he shouted, pointing toward the door. They obeyed, tripping over their feet as they went.

Prin stepped to the side to avoid them, shaking his head. He had told these very same servants to stay clear of the laboratory. They would have to be punished if they were to learn. Otherwise, Ulda would grow tired of their mistakes and use them in his experiments. There were already too few servants is it was. Prin did not relish the thought of losing more.

Extending his bony fingers, Ulda placed them on the smooth, glassy surface of the orb. Focusing his mind to Na'zora, an image of King Rykon came into view. The man was visibly angry, pounding his fists and shouting at the other men in the room. Ulda did not try to contain his laughter.

Aelryk had been a thorn in Ulda's side once, but the sorcerer had evened the score. No heroic death in battle had awaited the Na'zoran king. Instead, he had suffered long, lying in his bed and wasting away, all thanks to Ulda. No death could have been sweeter to watch.

His only regret was that he hadn't bound the king's soul. Looking upon his enemy for years to come would have brought immense joy to the sorcerer's world. It would have been a fun distraction from so much work. Alas, he had not the time or resources to send the necessary forces. In the end, he had settled for knowing that Aelryk had suffered and died, lying helpless and feeble.

Prin stood silently with his hands clenched behind his back. Peering slightly over his master's shoulder, he watched as images of Na'zora's countryside appeared within the orb. Over varying landscapes from cities to farms to forests, Ulda willed the orb to view the entire kingdom. Prin saw no signs of upheaval, nor any sign that the kingdom had been laid low by Ulda's hand. What was his master waiting for?

As if the sorcerer could read the servant's mind, he said, "Once the souls are brought back from the Vale, I can finalize my plans for the invasion of Na'zora. They will fall without much struggle." Continuing to stare into the orb, he pushed it farther, making his way to the Blue River.

Prin looked upon the river he had seen once before in the orb. Before it had been sparkling blue, the light dancing upon it as if in a dream. Now it was nothing but waste. More bog than river, Prin felt his lips turn downward and his body recoil at the sight of it.

Glancing over his shoulder, Ulda took note of the elf's expression. "Beautiful, isn't it?" he commented with a laugh. "The water is no longer plagued by the ancient spirit. I put an end to it, though I regret I couldn't capture its essence."

Ulda had learned to live with some failures. He simply wasn't prepared for such a struggle, and he could spend no more time studying the subject. Once he controlled the world, there would be plenty of time to perfect the technique. He would have the power of all life at his disposal, and that would lead him to his ultimate goal. Holding more power than the gods themselves was well within his grasp—so close he could almost robe himself in it.

Searching through the Vale, Ulda willed his orb to show him how River was faring after the destruction of his power source. An image of the elf, propped up in bed, appeared before the sorcerer. His wife and youngest daughter stood at his side. Smirking, Ulda thought, *How nice of them to keep him company.* Making note of River's pale complexion and his difficulty in raising his arms, Ulda concluded that he was more ill than he had expected. This was an added bonus for the wizard. He knew River's power would be drained, but he had expected him to recover quickly. After all, he was replenished by water, and that was all around him. The blow Ulda dealt had been much harder than expected, and this gave him great pleasure.

Tapping the orb with his finger, he pointed to the ailing elf. "It was easy to draw this one out of his safe little sanctuary in the forest," he said, without turning to look at his servant. "These sentimental types are all the same. They come running at the slightest inkling that someone needs their help."

"And that's why Aelryk had to die." Prin stated.

"Partially," Ulda replied in a casual tone. Sitting back in his seat, he rested his chin on his fingertips. "Aelryk deserved his fate. My punishment for him was long overdue. I hoped he would call for the aid of the Westerling Elves, and he did not disappoint. With River away, the Vale was left unprotected. His magical barriers are nothing for one as clever as me."

"Will they come after you once River is healed?" Prin asked, wondering what came next. His master was far too quiet about his intentions, and Prin liked to be prepared. He knew Ulda intended to take over several kingdoms in time, but he had never mentioned the possibility of a strike against his own tower at Ral'nassa. If he moved too slowly, those he wished to conquer might rise up to challenge him before he could reach their lands.

"It wouldn't do them any good," he replied, allowing the images in the orb to fade away. Swiveling in his seat, he turned his attention to the stacks of tomes on his table. Picking through the volumes, he said, "Swords and arrows are no match for me. Only River's magic posed any real threat, and now he may never recover."

Prin was risking his master's anger, but he had to know the answer to his next question. "Why send minions, Master? Why not just attack the Vale at a distance the same as you did the Spirit?"

Ulda waved a hand to dismiss the question. "It takes far too much energy, and binding the souls would be too difficult." Pausing, he looked up and stared at the wall in front of him. "Maybe the death of the Spirit will cause River to die of grief." Looking back down, he shook his head. "One can only guess. His origins are strange. I've found nothing like him in all my studies."

Prin understood perfectly. "You intend him to stand by powerless and watch as his home is destroyed and his children bound to your service."

"Indeed I do," Ulda replied. "Perhaps I'll even manage to get my hands on his true love. Wouldn't that be justice for my fallen army? The one he destroyed with the help of his elemental friends? I think I'd like that very much. I could find a special task for her."

Prin remained silent. He could already see what horrors his master might have in store for the elf woman. If her husband remained powerless, Ulda would likely bring him along to be studied as well.

"You're free to leave," Ulda said.

Without another word, Prin bowed to his master and left the room. The door clanged shut, and Prin stood at the ready outside it, should his master require his services.

Inside, Ulda turned his thoughts to Lenora and what experiments might be suitable for her. Regretting he had not instructed his troops to seek her out especially, he sighed and slumped down in his chair. It wouldn't surprise him if she put up a terrible fight. After all, she was a skilled healer with a deep store of magic. Whether she knew the appropriate spells to counter his own sorcerers he couldn't say. Glancing at his orb, he thought it might be best to contact the ship and tell them to look for her. Before doing so, his eye fell on a silver filigree coffer perched high on a shelf.

Smiling to himself, Ulda rose from his chair and climbed the wooden ladder to reach the box. Many long years ago he had loved a woman, possibly as much as River loved his mate. But Ulda was never good enough for her. No matter how hard he tried to impress her, she always refused his advances. She preferred fair-haired, doe-eyed boys who had no sense about them. Ulda was dark and quiet, his nose always stuck in a book. Every word he spoke only angered the lady he loved. She found him repulsive and told him so on several occasions. That had not stopped his love for her.

Lifting the coffer from its height, he gently carried it down the ladder and placed it on his desk. Smoothing out the creases in his chestnut-colored robe, he smiled softly at the box. Memories of the girl he loved flooded back to his mind. Her smooth olive skin and sparkling brown eyes were as lovely as the first day he'd met her. Never would she age or worry line her delicate features. She was his, for all eternity.

Opening the box, he peered inside where a large oval-shaped amethyst lay upon a cushion of white silk. Lifting the jewel in his hand, he gazed into the eyes of his love, her features twisted in torment. Her mouth opened as if to cry out, but no sound escaped her lips. Forever bound to the man she had rejected, her essence dwelt in agony inside the stone.

Looking upon the woman he had so adored, he said, "What do you say, love? Am I good enough for you now?" Tossing his head back, he laughed a deep, throaty laugh. "Things could have been different," he said. "Things could have been so different."

Chapter 13

Tucking her head beneath her father's arm, Alyra did her best impression of a crutch. Slowly the pair moved together down the stairs for the first time in days. River was feeling a bit stronger, but he still wasn't himself. Making every effort to hide how poorly he truly felt, he managed a weak smile for his youngest daughter.

Rushing off to the kitchen, Alyra prepared a variety of foods for her father, as well as the tea her mother had prescribed. Since she was unable to assist her brother and sister in preparing the Vale for a possible attack, she made the best of her abilities by acting as a nurse to her father.

When the girl returned with the food, Mel was standing near the fireplace, speaking in hushed tones

177

with River. Clearing her throat, she made her presence known. "Mother said he was to eat and keep his strength up," she said, giving Mel a cutting glance. "No talk of secret plans or anything else until he's eaten."

"Yes, my lady," River replied, pressing the cup to his lips. His heart swelled with love for his protective child, and he reached out an arm to draw her close to him. Squeezing her, he said, "Thank you. It's delicious." Picking at the small bowl of almonds she had brought, he popped a few in his mouth and smiled as he crunched them.

Hands on her hips, Alyra looked over at Mel, who threw his arms up in surrender. Turning away, he stared out of the window that faced the water. There had been no change to speak of, and the elves had tried every spell known to them to restore the water to its former state. Nothing had worked.

Lenora returned home with bundles of herbs piled high in her basket. A sigh of relief escaped her lips as she looked upon her life mate, who was finally sitting up and eating on his own. "I see our little nurse has been tending her duties well." She winked at her daughter as she set her basket down on the floor.

"Did the dryads have what you needed?" Alyra asked, rifling through the tender greens.

"They did," Lenora replied. "Could you take them upstairs for me?"

Alyra paused a moment and stared at her mother. She knew the task was simply an excuse to get her out of the room so the adults could talk, but she wasn't in the mood for an argument. Besides, she would be able to hear most of it from her secret spot in her mother's library. Snatching the basket from the floor, she bounded up the stairs without a word.

"How are you feeling?" Lenora asked River. "Be honest."

"I'm much better," he replied. "I am not at full strength, but that's to be expected." His eyes wandered to the scene outside the window.

"What's to be done?" Lenora asked.

"There is only one thing I can think of," River stated. "I will need Mel's help."

The sandy-haired elf turned away from the window and moved closer to the others. "Talk," he said.

"Master Ulda has bound the souls of great masters, absorbing their knowledge and acquiring their skills," River explained. "In essence, he has mastered all aspects of elemental magic."

That Ulda had done this came as no surprise to Mel. The sorcerer was obsessed with power, and stealing it from others seemed the fastest way to get it. Mel remained quiet and raised his eyebrows, awaiting further explanation.

"What is commonly known is there are four elements," River stated. "Great scholars have always debated about a fifth."

"They don't think it exists," Mel said with a shrug.

"That's because it isn't something they can touch," Lenora said. "They don't believe in things that aren't tangible."

"Precisely," River continued. "It is not an element that one can master by careful study. There is no college that teaches such magic."

Mel held up a hand. "You're hinting at something, and you want me to guess it. Just spit it out already."

"I believe Ulda has mastered the fifth element," River stated flatly. "There is no other way he could have defeated the Spirit."

"So how do we defeat him?" Mel asked. "What element do we need?"

"The other four," Lenora replied, looking at the floor. She knew what this would mean for her life mate.

River nodded his agreement. "Four elementals could combine forces to defeat Ulda."

"Great," Mel replied. "Where do we find them?"

With a grin, River replied, "We have two right here. You and me."

Shaking his head, Mel gave a sarcastic laugh. "I'm not an elemental." With a mocking wag of his finger, he said, "You've lost your mind."

"I saw an earth elemental once, centuries ago," Lenora said in a quiet voice. "It was a remarkable creature." With heaviness, she added, "Even the dryads have not seen one in many years. They are all too deeply asleep now, locked inside the earth."

"That's why Mel will have to represent earth," River said, looking into Mel's emerald green eyes. "Will you do it?"

Mel stumbled on his words a moment, but finally managed to ask, "How? I'm not an elemental."

"You have a deeper connection to the earth than any elf I've met," River said.

"Why not use one of the dryads?" Mel wondered. "Surely they are more connected and stronger than me when it comes to earth magic."

"The dryads cannot leave the forest," Lenora reminded him. "You will have to travel to Ral'nassa."

"You have more strength than you know," River told him. "I cannot do this alone. All of Nōl'Deron, including your forest, is in danger."

Mel went silent for a moment. There was nothing he wanted more from life than to protect his people in the Forests of Viera. It was a beautiful place, unlike any other. Only the Vale rivaled it in beauty. When magic first awoke in him, he wondered why it had chosen him. Then he had discovered it was a way to bring his people back to the ways of old. His connection to the earth only deepened over the years as he honed his talents and drew power inside him. If Ulda was threatening his home, he wouldn't stand by and watch. Even if it led him to his death, Mel would not refuse the fight. "I will go with you," he stated.

"I'm glad to hear it," River replied.

"Now where do we get air and fire?" Mel asked. "Wait, I'm going to burn things and you're going to blow on them." He grinned, amused by his own joke. His audience, however, only frowned. "Okay, seriously," he said. "Are there other elementals around, or will we be rounding up a few more elves?"

"Air dwells above us in the mountains," River replied. "But she is not an elf. She's a dwarf."

"Now I've heard everything," Mel said, shaking his head. "I didn't know dwarves could learn magic at all, and I certainly didn't know they mastered the elements."

"Most of them don't," River said with a shrug. "Kaiya is different."

"She must be," Mel replied. "How do we get in touch with her?"

"You climb up the waterfall," Lenora replied, a broad smile on her face. She remembered a day many years ago when she had done just that at River's side.

"You're joking," Mel said.

"Only slightly," River replied. "The fastest way to Kaiya would indeed be to go up the waterfall. Unfortunately, I don't have the strength to alter it for you."

"He turned it into a staircase once," Lenora said. "We marched up it like it was the most ordinary thing in the world."

"I'm not a mountain climber," Mel said. "If you can't do what you did before, how do you expect me to go and fetch this Kaiya?"

"You're a master of earth magic," River reminded him. "The cliff face is naught but rock. You can command it."

Mel clenched his jaw, not wanting to repeat himself. River had almost certainly lost his mind. Mel never had such an ability.

"When you stop doubting your abilities, you'll see that it's indeed possible," River said, his voice sincere.

Mel sighed and thought, *More of that Westerling Elf "believe in yourself" magical style.* "All right, fine," he said. "I'll command the mountain to take me to Kaiya. Should I fetch fire on my way back?"

River's confident expression grew dark. "There is only one person I can think of to represent fire. I will have to convince him to come with us."

Lenora placed her hands over her mouth to stifle a gasp.

"Who is it?" Mel asked.

"Telorithan," River replied.

Mel startled at the mention of the sorcerer's name. "He is a murderer," he said. "Our people avoid him at all costs. He is extremely dangerous. Even the slightest affront is answered with death. I would not trust him to help us."

"This cause is as much his own as it is ours," River explained. "I will go to fetch him, and you and Kaiya will come with me."

Mel didn't like the sound of that, but he nodded anyway. River seemed to know what he was talking about, so Mel didn't question him further. Perhaps the three of them together would pose enough threat that Telorithan would do them no harm. Otherwise, all River's planning would be in vain.

A scuffling on the floor above them caught the trio's attention.

"A mouse, no doubt," River said, his eyes twinkling with mischief.

Lenora pursed her lips and crossed her arms. "A mouse who likes to listen to things that don't concern her."

River patted his life mate's arm. "It concerns us all, my love," he said. "There is no harm in what she's heard."

"I guess it's time for me to get going," Mel said with a sigh. "After all, I've got a mountain to climb."

* * * * *

Stepping out into the chilly air, Mel realized that the temperature in the Vale wasn't right. Winter never came to this land, and though it wasn't yet as cold as it was back home, he was well aware of the change in climate. Whatever Ulda was planning, it went much deeper than simply ridding himself of an ancient water spirit.

Making his way to the riverbank, Mel noticed stacks of nets neatly folded and placed above the water line. With the absence of dead fish, Mel knew that the elves had been hard at work removing the carcasses from the river. The smell remained but at a much more tolerable level.

As he approached the water, he saw that the top inch or so was clear, the gray filth having settled somewhat. His better judgment warned him not to get too much of it on him, as it likely still contained the potent poison that had killed the fish. Looking up at the waterfall that fed into the river, he deemed the water flowing in to be pristine. The beauty of the falls was not diminished by the tainted water below.

According to River's instructions, the rock formation behind the waterfall was where Mel needed to climb to access the dwarf village above. Looking around, Mel wondered how best to get to the falls without immersing himself in the water. His eyes fell on a small boat floating untethered only an arm's length away. It hugged the bank unnaturally, as if it had no desire to remain in the water.

Climbing inside the tiny vessel, Mel was thankful to keep his feet dry. The Westerling Elves built sturdy crafts, and this one had no leaks. Slowly paddling toward the rocks, he noticed the boulders at the waterfall's base were surrounded by clean water. Ulda's evil had not been able to overcome the force of nature. Looking up to the top of the falls, Mel smiled. It was an amazing sight to behold, and the scent of fresh water gave him a feeling of serenity.

Preparing to be pummeled by the falling water, Mel hunched his shoulders as he rowed beneath it. The tumbling water landed on him with force, drenching him with a surprisingly warm shower. Though he was rather wet, the experience had not been the painful one he expected. If anything, he felt rejuvenated by its power.

Finding a sturdy platform of black rock, Mel pulled himself out of his boat and stood on the ledge. The rocks above him were slick with water. Grabbing at one, his hand immediately slipped away. *Glad I kept my feet on the ground,* he thought. With a sigh, he remembered that he was no mountain climber. *Trees are so much easier than rocks.* As if a light had gone off in his head, he realized what he needed to do.

Focusing his energy into the ground, Mel reached deep into the earth beneath his feet. Summoning his magic, he concentrated on the wall, holding his breath as vines sprouted upon the surface of the rock. Closing his eyes, he focused deeper, forcing them to grow thick and sturdy. When he opened his eyes, he beheld vines so thick they had grown bark. Tugging at one, he nodded approvingly at his own effort. "These will do just fine," he said, complimenting himself. Since becoming a shaman, the earth-magic spells he could cast sometimes surprised him. This was one of those times.

Scampering up the vines with the agility of one who has climbed trees his entire life, Mel found himself quickly nearing the top. A faint scratching sound came from beneath him, and he paused to look down and investigate. He saw nothing. Deciding he was growing paranoid with all the evil sorcerer talk, he shrugged it off and continued his ascent.

Within minutes, Mel's hands landed upon a plateau that was wide enough to stand on. Pulling himself to the top, he planted his feet firmly on the hard-packed ground. To his delight, a narrow path stretched before him in the brown grass of winter. The path had mostly been overgrown, but at one time, it had obviously been used with some frequency.

Heading down the path that would lead to the dwarf village, Mel once again heard a noise, this time similar to a small animal in the grass. Glancing over his shoulder, he saw nothing. Shaking his head, he dismissed the sound. It was likely some creature in search of food. His senses were always heightened after pulling large amounts of magic, so he did his best to ignore whatever it was.

Not far ahead, Mel saw smoke rising in faint silver lines. As he continued forward, more smoke came into view, rising high from the chimneys on the homes of the dwarves. Much quicker than expected, he had reached the dwarf village, where a master of air magic dwelt.

Chapter 14

Looking toward the dwarf village, Mel counted dozens of homes clustered near each other, as well as a rather large marketplace. Despite the cold air, the village bustled with activity. The smell of fresh-baked goods wafted on the air, his stomach rumbling in response. Hammers rang out from the smithy, and black smoke spewed from the forge. As always, the dwarves were hard at work crafting metals, a specialty among their kind.

At first Mel went unnoticed by the busy citizens, but eventually he started receiving some glances. One woman stared intently at the elf, tripping over her own feet and nearly tumbling to the ground. Mel stifled a laugh and looked away, taking in the sturdy dwarven architecture. All the buildings were crafted of stone, not at all like the huts his people lived in. Unlike Mel's clan, these people had no intention of moving in search of better hunting for the winter.

Mel walked through the dwarf village with his head held high. At only five feet in height, he rarely had the opportunity to look down at anyone. All of the dwarves stood at least a head shorter than him, and that gave him a sense of pride. He knew it probably made him a jerk to feel that way, but he didn't care. Being the tall one in the room was a nice change, and he planned to enjoy it.

"Elk skin?" a husky voice asked.

Looking to his right, Mel's eyes fell on a stocky dwarf dressed in a thick wool tunic. In his hand was a stout needle and a leather pouch, to which he sewed a strip of sleek, brown fur.

"Excuse me?" Mel asked.

"Elk skin, I said," the dwarf repeated. "Your clothes. The leather looks soft." The man stepped forward and reached out for Mel's sleeve. "Am I right?"

"It is," Mel replied, taking a step back. "Are you a tailor?"

"Of sorts," the dwarf replied with a shrug. "Ard's the name." With a wide smile on his lips, he extended a thick hand toward the elf. Grasping Mel's hand, he squeezed it with a firm grip. "You here to trade?" Ard looked around for the rest of the elves. "Are you alone?"

"Yep, just little old me," Mel said and immediately bit his lip. Not exactly a joke he should be making in front of dwarves, but it was an expression he used often among humans.

"Where are your goods?" Ard asked, puzzled. Mel had no pack or a cart. Woodland Elves never made the journey into the mountains without numerous items to trade.

"I'm not here to trade," Mel explained. "I'm looking for someone." Quickly, he added, "A friend of mine." Though he'd never met Kaiya, he didn't want to sound like he had a score to settle. If he was to find her, he needed to get the dwarves talking, not have them clam up in defense of their own.

"Friend, huh?" Ard replied. "What's the name?"

Not sure which question the dwarf had meant to ask, the elf replied, "*My* name's Mel, and I'm *looking* for Kaiya."

"Kaiya?" Ard repeated, laughing. "She's not here."

She probably flew away on a gust of wind, Mel thought. He rolled his eyes, annoyed that he'd made the trip at all. Hoping she hadn't traveled too far, he asked, "Do you have any idea where she is?"

Ard grinned. "'Course I do. She's at her house a short walk outside of town. Rarely leaves her farm, that one."

Relieved, Mel said, "Thanks. Can you point me in her direction?"

"Sure," Ard replied, pointing. "Just follow that path. It'll lead you right to her."

"How do I know which house is hers?"

"It's the only one in that direction," Ard replied with a shrug. "Sheep, goats, you can't miss it."

"Appreciate it," Mel said with a nod.

Turning away from the village, he followed the stone and dirt path that led to Kaiya's farm. Shaking his head, he tried to suppress the thought that River's most powerful ally was nothing more than a farmer. The path wound on, ranging from completely overgrown to barren in various patches. It appeared Kaiya didn't travel this route often.

Finally Mel spotted a quaint little farmhouse in the distance. Its construction was simple, but the land surrounding it was breathtaking. It grew fertile and green as if the seasons stood still, providing this land with a permanence of springtime, just as the Vale had been. Mel marveled at the sight of apple trees in full bloom and cornstalks taller than himself. *I guess it's true that masters of air can control the weather,* he decided.

To the side of the house stood a woman with violet hair, a single streak of silver weaving its way through the strands. She wore a plain ivory blouse and leather breeches, and carried a metal bucket in her hands. Three black dogs pranced playfully at her feet. Was this Kaiya, or was this some farmhand she had hired? Mel moved closer to her, wondering how such an average-looking woman could be so powerful.

It wouldn't be long before Mel found out. From nowhere, a sudden tightness hit his chest, squeezing the breath from his lungs. Looking up, he saw Kaiya staring straight at him, her arms resting at her side. The spell she cast held him firmly in place, but she made no outward gesture to indicate she was using magic, save for the silver glow in her eyes.

Projecting with his mind, Mel said, *I yield.* At once the spell was lifted, and the elf breathed freely. The dogs moved closer to him, stopping halfway between the dwarf and the elf, barking as if they were about to defend against an attack.

Kaiya approached, her eyes intent on the intruder. Though he didn't know how, he was sure she was reading his thoughts. He could feel her penetrating his mind with her own, but he was powerless to stop her. In her he sensed more power than he had ever encountered.

"You can just ask, you know," he said coldly. "You don't have to pry into my mind."

Kaiya dropped the spell and narrowed her eyes. "I'm sorry, Master Elf," she said. "The wind brings ill tidings, and there are strange creatures about in the land. Forgive my suspicious nature." Reaching out a hand, she offered it to Mel in friendship.

Shaking the woman's hand, Mel replied, "You don't know the half of it."

The dogs continued to bark until Kaiya demanded they stop. "To the porch!" she commanded, pointing to the house. The dogs obeyed without a second thought. "You are a friend of River?"

"I am," Mel replied, a little surprised. She must have found the information in his thoughts. "My name's Mel. Are you Kaiya?"

"Yes," she replied. "And the girl? Who is she?"

Wrinkling his brown, Mel asked, "What girl?"

Pointing toward a tree, Kaiya said, "That girl. The one who's hiding behind the tree."

Mel turned in time to see Alyra stepping sheepishly from behind the tree trunk. Dumbfounded, he asked, "How did you get here?"

Stepping forward, Alyra replied, "I was afraid you couldn't convince Kaiya to come with you, so I came along just in case."

With Alyra so close, Kaiya recognized her instantly. "You're Lenora and River's youngest," she said with a smile. "You were a tiny little thing the last time I saw you."

Alyra blushed, embarrassed that she did not recognize the dwarf.

"Don't worry," Kaiya said. "You were too little to remember me." She turned her attention back to Mel. "Why have you come here?"

"River asked me to," he explained. "Ulda has attacked the Vale, and the Spirit has been killed. He has a plan to stop him, but it requires all four elements."

Kaiya dipped her head in understanding. "He needs four elements to conquer the fifth. These are dangerous times."

Mel wondered how she could know so much, but he swallowed the question, accepting that she possessed powers he lacked.

"My father is ill," Alyra blurted. "He needs help, and my mother's medicine isn't enough." She felt a little ashamed to admit it, but it was the truth. If Lenora could have healed him, she would have done it already. Kaiya was the most powerful sorceress Alyra had ever heard of. If anyone could help him, it was her.

"I see," Kaiya replied. "You can help me with that." She gave the girl a crooked smile, attempting to keep the mood playful. The child was already worried enough. "Let me fetch my bag," she said before disappearing inside her house.

Mel looked over at Alyra, who was wringing her hands and looking at the ground. "Your parents are probably worried sick," he said.

The girl did not look up at him.

"Were you following me the whole time?" he asked.

"No," she replied, still looking away. "I was in front of you for a while."

Mel shook his head. He could never understand the children in his clan, so why should this child be any different? For such small people, they certainly had working minds of their own.

Kaiya reappeared with a large leather bag slung across her back. "All set," she said. To Alyra, she said,

"Can you help me collect some medicine for your father?"

Alyra nodded quickly, eager to help.

"Good," Kaiya said with a wink. "We'll just head to the small creek where the snow melts from the mountain tops. The water there is special, and it will help your father."

The young elf girl rushed forward, grabbing Kaiya firmly and squeezing her. "Thank you," she said with tears gleaming in her eyes.

"Your father will be fine, Alyra. I promise." Motioning for Mel to follow, Kaiya led her guests northward, away from her farm. "The Blue River has its source in these mountains," she explained as they walked. "The water there is pristine."

"That explains the waterfall," Mel commented. "It wasn't filthy like the river water below. It has been tainted by Ulda's magic."

"Maybe we can fix that too," Kaiya said. She had next to no experience with water magic, but if there was a way to cleanse the water without controlling it, Kaiya would find a way. It was the least she could do for an old friend.

Arriving at a small, rocky creek, Kaiya fished in her bag for a vial. "Take this," she told Alyra. "Fill it with water." She handed the vial to the girl, who eagerly grabbed it from her hand.

Alyra stepped carefully over the slippery rocks, her toes feeling the cold water through her soft slippers. The water trickled down the side of a large rock formation, and Alyra looked up to see the snow-covered caps of the Wrathful Mountains. It amazed her that such a small trickle could turn into the falls and river below where she made her home.

Holding the vial as close to the wall as she could, she dipped it in the water. At only a few inches deep, it took a moment to fill the entire bottle, but she didn't want to retrieve too little. She waited patiently until it was full and then placed the stopper firmly in place. With pride, she held the vial in front of her. "Got it!" she said with a smile.

"Great," Kaiya said warmly. Taking the vial, she placed it safely in her bag. "Now let's get you home before your parents skin Mel alive." She chuckled softly, as did the girl.

Mel scowled. "I didn't drag her up here," he stated, crossing his arms. With a shrug, he added, "The kid's a nuisance." Though he tried to keep a straight face, he couldn't help but laugh. He was a master of earth magic who was supposed to be more in touch with his surroundings than any other, but he had been outwitted by a clever child. Suspecting there was more to her ability to stay hidden than she had admitted, he slapped the girl on the shoulder and nodded approvingly. "Careful or you'll make a fine little criminal someday."

Giggling, Alyra led the way back to the path. Making a sharp turn, she changed course to avoid the town and take them directly to the overhang where they could climb down.

Suspiciously, Kaiya asked, "Have you been here before?"

Alyra shook her head. "Nope. I'm just good with directions."

Kaiya dared to peek inside the child's mind and discovered a three-dimensional map of the area engrained in her memory. Marveling that the child could learn so much about her home's geography in one visit, Kaiya knew Alyra was indeed a talented elf. Her magic was locked inside, buried until she was physically capable of handling it. Although the dwarf could see the girl's mind, she was unsure exactly what form the magic would take. It pleased her to be in the dark for once. The average mind was far too open, and she preferred a bit of a mystery.

"This is the spot," Alyra announced as they reached the plateau. Nimbly she clutched at the rocks, eager to lead the way down.

Mel rushed to her, shouting, "Wait!" The vines he had summoned were still in place, and he tugged on them to be sure they were still strong enough to bear the weight. Satisfied with their strength, he said, "Let me go first." Though the vines appeared as they were before, he didn't want a child slipping while he was clinging to a vine and unable to catch her.

Alyra waited until Mel was halfway down to begin her descent. Her small hands clutched firmly at the living rope, and she moved with a graceful ease.

Not to be outdone, Kaiya's eyes flashed silver. Gliding to the bottom on a soft current of air, she grinned at her companions as she passed them.

Alyra stared open-mouthed, and Mel gave a sullen, pouty look.

With a laugh, Kaiya said, "Climb aboard!" Ascending slightly to gather the others, she allowed them onto her barely visible air boat.

As they reached the riverbank, Mel noticed the rowboat he had taken was tied to the shore. "I guess it's a good thing you came, or we'd have to wade through that." He pointed to the mucky water.

"I see," Kaiya said, looking deep into the river. Rummaging through her bag, she retrieved the water Alyra had collected and pulled the stopper out with her teeth.

"That's for my father!" Alyra shouted, her voice thin. She reached out a hand as if to take it away from the sorceress.

"I need only a drop," Kaiya reassured her. "I also need Mel's help."

Nodding, Mel moved to Kaiya's side. "What are you going to do?"

"I'm going to clean the water," she said. Glancing at Alyra, she explained, "I can't make it what it was. Only River can do that. But I can render it safe for drinking, and banish the remaining evil."

"How can I help?" Mel wondered. If he'd had the inclination he could do something useful, he'd have done it already.

"River is far too weak to help, and it's too difficult a task for someone who isn't a master of water." She handed him the vial. "But if we work together, we can purify the water with air and earth."

Mel understood. Tipping the vial slightly, he placed a drop of the water in the river. Sinking to his hands and knees, he connected himself physically to the earth. Reaching in with his mind, he pulled the magic from the earth's depths, forcing it into the water.

Kaiya spread her hands skyward, filling the once-blue sky with thick, gray clouds. The air around her warmed, the temperature rising to uncomfortable levels. Alyra stepped away, her heart pounding in her ears. Though frightened, she could not take her eyes off the spectacle.

Summoning the power of the wind, Kaiya focused her energy into the water. All around her the air swirled, her loose hair dancing on the breeze. With a quick motion, she lowered her right palm to hover above the water's surface. A bolt of lightning struck the water, followed quickly by a second.

Mel wasn't expecting the loud crash it created and nearly lost concentration. Refocusing his energy away from the ringing in his ears, he forced the magic to rise from the earth. When he opened his eyes, the water was clear.

"It's all right," Kaiya said softly to Alyra. "Come and see."

Alyra stepped forward, her hands clasped tightly at the center of her chest. Cautiously she peered into the depths. "I can see the bottom!" she shouted, her breath escaping. "How?"

A wide smile spread across Kaiya's lips. "Magic, darling."

Chapter 15

Bursting through the door to her home, Alyra announced, "She's here!" Running to her father's side, she told him, "Kaiya has come back with us." Pointing to the door as Kaiya stepped inside, Alyra's face beamed with pride.

"You weren't supposed to go into the mountains," River scolded, suppressing a smile.

Lenora crossed her arms and pursed her lips as she looked at her life mate. "No, she wasn't," she stated. "It's too dangerous for you to run off whenever you like, Alyra."

Alyra hung her head. "I know," she said.

Kaiya stepped forward to greet her old friends. "It's good to see you both." First, she reached for Lenora and squeezed her tightly. The trio had been friends for centuries, though they went long periods without seeing each other. As she approached River, she could sense his lack of magical strength. Hugging him, she said, "How are you, my friend?"

"I've been better," he answered honestly. There was no point in hiding his illness from Kaiya. She was far too intuitive to be deceived.

Kaiya took a seat next to Lenora. "I hear a sorcerer by the name of Ulda is giving you some trouble. Mel filled me in on your plan to be rid of him."

"More like she scanned it out of my brain," Mel said, crossing his arms.

Lenora chuckled slightly. "Tell me, Kaiya, have you ever managed to find that air elemental you were looking for?"

Her eyes twinkling, Kaiya replied, "It took many years, but I finally realized I didn't need to find one."

River's lips turned up into a slight smile as he patted his friend on the back. "You've grown so much as a sorceress since our first meeting." His mind flashed back to the time when Kaiya was an outcast among her people, and they distrusted her magic. Now she was a well-respected leader among the dwarves. Her council was sought by kings and commoners alike.

Mel took a seat and turned his attention to Kaiya. "Won't the dwarves be in need of your protection? Ulda could just as likely attack there as here."

"Ulda probably considers us dwarves too far beneath him to take notice," Kaiya replied. "And the dwarves remain oblivious to the world around them and won't worry about him until he's on their doorstep. It's how it always goes."

"Your people have vast resources that a man like Ulda would covet," Mel cautioned. "It might have been best to warn them."

Kaiya waved a hand, dismissing the comment. "If anyone sets their sights on my people, I'll be the first to know."

Mel didn't argue. The dwarf held powers he was unfamiliar with, and he wasn't sure he wanted a demonstration of all of them.

A sharp knock sounded at the door, and Alyra rushed to open it. Isandra stepped inside.

"You know you don't have to knock," Alyra said, crossing her arms and shaking her head.

"I no longer dwell here," Isandra stated. "It's the polite thing to do." Marching away from her sister, she announced, "Representatives from Na'zora have arrived. They wish to speak with you, Father."

Slowly, River rose from his feet and searched for his balance. Lenora stood in a flash and grabbed his arm to steady him. Gently he patted her hand, grateful for the assistance. Though he seemed to be recovering, he was still having trouble with his strength.

"Wait," Mel said, rising from his seat. "How do we know this isn't a trick?"

"I sense no malice," Kaiya replied.

Isandra looked at the dwarf curiously. To her father, she said, "I have checked the men thoroughly. They are what they claim to be." Glancing at Mel, she dared him to question her skills as protector of the Vale.

"I know you have," River replied. Following his daughter, he stepped outside to greet the visitors assembled at the center of the village. A large meeting area had been constructed there, consisting of several long wooden benches and a central fire pit. Though the council house was the preferred meeting place for matters concerning safety, these guests were too important to hide away. The entire village had come to view them and hear their words.

"Lord River," General Aldryg said, extending a hand to the elf. "I am General Aldryg. I have come on the orders of King Rykon to provide assistance to your people. He feared for your personal safety."

"I thank you, but I am quite safe," River replied. "Rykon could have used the ring to contact me and save you such a long journey."

"He was unable to use it," Aldryg explained.

River looked down at the ground, realizing why the ring had failed to obey Rykon's command. Without the Spirit, there was no one to convey the king's words to River.

"There is also another matter," the general continued. "King Rykon would like to form an alliance that our peoples might march on Ral'nassa together."

"We would be honored," River replied.

"Do you have more than the hundred men you brought with you?" Isandra demanded. "Your numbers won't make much difference unless fifty of them are mages." She was not the kind of woman to keep her opinions to herself. Whether she offended the general was irrelevant.

"My lady, I assure you we have an adequate army waiting to join us in Na'zora," the general replied. "I brought the number of men I thought I might need to fight my way here."

Isandra nodded, looking through the ranks of the troops. "They look sturdy," she stated. "I would be pleased to fight next to them."

Aldryg added, "We do have some well-trained mages at home as well. They did not join me for this trip."

"I think we've got enough magic here to cover it," Kaiya said with a grin.

Tired of holding back her feelings, Lenora spoke up. "My life mate is not as healthy as he was the last time Na'zora needed our help. He has been attacked by Ulda, and the Spirit who guides him has been slain. River is ill, and your army will need to do more of the work this time." There was a hint of anger in her voice. This general had not bothered to ask after River's health, even though he was visibly unwell. Lenora would not allow them to pressure him into attempting magic that could only deplete him further.

River hugged her to his side. "She is a healer," he explained. "I assure you I'll be quite well once we reach the ocean."

Lenora sighed and looked away. He was keeping secrets again to spare her feelings, and she hated it. It was best to have the truth and deal with it rather than be sheltered with false hope. Instead of arguing, she maintained her silence. Before they would depart, she would speak with him alone and know the truth.

Kaiya stepped forward and motioned for River to kneel down to her level. Placing her hands upon his head, she closed her eyes and focused energy into her magical stores. Spreading silver magic over his body, she transferred power to her friend. When he stood, his eyes flashed with a silver-blue sheen.

"That should help," she said. "Don't use it all in one place."

"Your assistance is most welcome, my friend," he replied, laying a hand on her shoulder. To Lenora, he said, "You see, I have all the help I shall need." He squeezed her tightly and kissed the top of her golden head.

Lenora's eyes glistened with tears, but she fought them back. With help from both Kaiya and Mel, she knew her husband would indeed make it to the ocean. What would happen when he arrived there remained a mystery. Until now, there had never been a day when the Spirit who gave River his life had been absent. Without its guidance, River might falter.

Lenora had run out of ideas for healing her life mate, but Kaiya and Mel were skilled with elemental magic. Perhaps with their help she would discover a way to cure him entirely. She could only hope there was time. Otherwise, she might lose him before she could find the cure. With Ulda threatening their every move, he would have to be dealt with first. Lenora dreaded what might happen in the confrontation, but she buried her worry inside and put on a brave face.

"We should discuss our plans for the invasion of Ral'nassa," Isandra said.

Aldryg looked to River for approval. He had been told to converse with River, not a subordinate. The general was unsure who was in charge of the elven army.

"That's a good idea," River said. "This is my daughter Isandra," he told the general. "She is a leader among our soldiers, and she is quite knowledgeable when it comes to battle."

Isandra inclined her head slightly to the general. It was clear from his expression he hadn't expected to find a woman in charge of a regiment. Isandra thought Aldryg's people were foolish to refuse their women the chance to fight. The more swords, the better. Women were just as vulnerable in times of war as men.

The Westerling Elves allowed all who wished to learn the art of swordplay to learn it, though most preferred a less violent course of study. Isandra had excelled in her training as a warrior, and she craved the chance to defend her people.

"Very well then," the general replied. Extending a hand to Isandra, he introduced himself. "I am General Aldryg," he said. "It's a pleasure."

Isandra ignored his gesture. Glancing at her father, she said, "We will sit and talk." The group moved to a set of benches crafted from the fallen limbs of silver trees. They had broken from the massive trees ages ago but were still perfectly strong, allowing the elves to use them without damaging any of the trees. Their surfaces were smooth, with adornments of leaves carved into them. Even when crafting practical objects, the elves took extra care to make them beautiful.

Each member of the party took a seat, with Mel seating himself cross-legged on the ground. Kaiya and Lenora sat on either side of River, both keeping a close watch on his demeanor. Isandra sat across form General Aldryg, her gaze intent.

"Tell me of Na'zora's navy, General," she demanded. "Our journey will require us to cross many miles of ocean."

Aldryg cleared his throat before speaking. "Na'zora hasn't much of a navy," he began. "King Aelryk's father had dreamed of building a great one, but when Aelryk took the throne, that dream died. He was far more interested in peace."

"We could wait for Ulda to come to us," Mel suggested. "I doubt it will be long before he does so."

"That would require us to prepare on two fronts," Isandra replied. "Both the Vale and Na'zora's coast would be vulnerable. We don't know what he's planning."

River nodded in agreement. "My daughter is right," he said. "We must take the fight to Ulda and face him on his own turf."

Aldryg's eyes darted from one to the other. "Na'zora doesn't have enough ships for our combined armies," he admitted. "In fact, we have enough ships for only about half of us."

"How do you plan to invade without warships?" Isandra asked, raising her voice. "Did you come here thinking that we would provide this? Would you sail from our coast with only a hundred of your men?"

"Not at all," the general replied. "Sailing from Na'zora would make more sense. It would be a much shorter journey by sea."

"But you don't have the ships," Mel added, leaning back against a stump. "What was your king planning to do about that?"

Letting out a deep breath, he replied, "King Rykon would gladly build the needed ships, but that would take years. He is eager to bring justice to his father's murderer. I believe he would swim if he had to."

"That didn't answer my question," Mel pointed out.

River sighed. "King Rykon was counting on me to handle that," he said. "He's well aware of what occurred during our last encounter with Ulda. I raised the sea with the help of the elementals."

Lenora placed a loving hand against her life mate's chest. "You don't have the strength," she said. "He can't expect it of you now."

"Once I'm near the ocean, I will have the strength I need," he replied. "I will summon the elementals, and they will help us."

"So we're going to ride on a tidal wave to Ral'nassa?" Mel asked, narrowing his eyes. "That won't do much for keeping in formation." He chuckled to himself but quickly became silent when he noticed no one else was laughing. Shaking his head, he said, "It was only a joke."

"This is no time for laughing," Isandra replied sternly.

River raised a hand to silence them. "I will summon the elementals as we go. The army will walk across the ocean to face Ulda."

Aldryg stared at him wide-eyed. He could not think of a suitable response. In his mind, he could only imagine what such an event would look like.

"Will you have the strength by then?" Kaiya asked, her brow wrinkling with concern. If she was to arrive strong enough to fight, she wouldn't be able to help him replenish his magic.

"The ocean will help," he said confidently. "I will have the strength."

"Then it's settled," Isandra declared. "We will begin preparations immediately. Ulda's days are numbered." Though it was unlikely he could be cut down with a sword, Isandra hoped she would have the opportunity to face him personally. There was no one in the world she would rather kill than the man who had laid such an attack against her father and the Spirit.

"You still haven't explained to Kaiya and me exactly what it is we're going to do," Mel said to River. "It sounded like you had something specific in mind. I might need time to practice." Knowing he was not as powerful as River or Kaiya, he could be at a disadvantage in this fight. After all, he had never used his powers to harm anything. His years as a shaman focused only on healing the forest and seeing to the needs of his people.

"You'll know what to do when the time comes," River assured him. "It will come naturally to you."

Mel wasn't so sure. With a sigh, he looked at Kaiya. Her face showed the same confidence as River. Maybe she would plant the correct spells in his mind a minute or two before the fight. Still, he didn't like being kept in the dark. Deciding to remain silent for now, he would demand a better explanation once the army was moving out.

"We should also discuss what skills your soldiers possess," Isandra said. "It's best to decide where to put them while we march in case we are attacked en route."

"An excellent idea," the general replied.

Lenora jumped to her feet, interrupting the pair. "There's trouble," she said, her eyes wide. "Rogin needs our help."

Chapter 16

Standing high upon his lookout in the forest canopy, Rogin noticed a slight movement in the limbs lower to the ground. A faint grunting sound found its way to his ears as he strained his hearing to determine what creature was approaching. What came into view took him by surprise. Not one, but dozens of tall, blue-furred beasts ran through the forest, knocking limbs aside and trampling the earth. Shrieking sounds from unseen beasts pierced the air as Rogin descended from his post. The Vale was under attack.

The blast of a horn told Rogin that other scouts had spotted the invaders, and his troops were already assembling to defend the Vale. Reaching the ground, he found himself face to face with a black-and-orange-striped creature that was coming through the brush.

Drawing back instinctively, Rogin put nearly a foot of distance between himself and his opponent. Swiping its massive claw, it attempted to slaughter the elf before a fight could ensue. Rogin was too fast. He moved gracefully, arching his body to avoid the claws. Drawing his sword, he thrust it at the creature.

Proving itself an agile opponent, the creature danced around Rogin, avoiding each swipe of the elf's sword. His back now against the rope ladder, Rogin grabbed on, hoping to gain some height on the monster. Instead of following him, the tiger hybrid crouched low, staying out of the elf's reach. A low growl escaped its throat as it prepared to pounce.

Rogin kept a close eye on the creature's legs as he continued to ascend the ladder. If he could reach the top, he could switch to his bow and, hopefully, take it down in one shot. Unfortunately, he had no idea how high these things could jump.

As he neared the top, he saw the characteristic wiggle that preceded the pounce. In a flash, the tiger's massive claws lunged toward Rogin's face, the full weight of the monster behind them. With little time to react, he reached for the dagger that was sheathed in his belt. In one fluid motion, he drew the dagger and plunged it in the tiger's throat, spilling its deep-red blood. Rogin hurried down the ladder, which was now slick with blood.

Keeping low through the brush, the elf moved forward in hopes of uniting with his regiment. Battle cries rang in his ears, both elven and unknown. Continuing at a steady pace, he soon came into view of the battle. In the clearing he saw giant spiders, more of the tiger beasts, and the blue-furred wolfmen he had seen many years before. The continued rustling from the trees suggested more soldiers might be on the way. Positioning himself to join the attack, his attention was drawn by a massive shadow circling above him.

Looking up at a set of reptilian wings, Rogin's heart leapt to his throat. Above him was a wyvern with a robed figure seated on its back. Opening its mouth to expose rows of jagged teeth, the wyvern let out a high, piercing shriek. Rogin resisted the urge to cover his ears and instead drew his bow.

Taking aim at what he suspected was the wyvern's heart, the elf loosed an arrow. The pointed tip found its mark but glanced off against the beast's ironlike scales. Crying out in anger, the wyvern circled around to get a better look at its opponent. Fixing its talons, it dove from the sky, determined to eliminate the threat below.

Crouching low to the ground, Rogin waited until the talons were almost upon him before rolling to his left to avoid them. The wyvern circled, spurred on by its master, and positioned itself for a second attack. Rogin loosed another arrow, this time aimed at its head. Before it could hit its target, the sorcerer intervened, blasting the arrow to splinters midair.

Rogin drew his sword and stood his ground as the wyvern moved in for a third attack. The sorcerer threw a blast of light toward the elf, who barely had time to dodge. Losing his balance, Rogin fell to the ground but quickly righted himself. Flying low, the wyvern targeted the elf's head with its thick, scaly tail. Rogin attempted to avoid the blow, but he underestimated the width of his opponent's barbed tail. It hit his back hard, forcing him to his knees and knocking the sword from his hand.

As the elf reached for his sword, the wyvern swooped again, grabbing his midsection in its grisly talons. Crying out from the crushing pain, Rogin wasted the air from his lungs, allowing the beast to squeeze harder. Desperately trying to catch his breath before the life was squeezed out of him, he pulled at the talons with his hand to free himself. It was no use. The wyvern was far stronger than the elf. Reaching for his dagger, Rogin secured the blade in his hand and plunged it into one of the slender toes. Screeching in pain, the wyvern released its prey, dropping him into the trees below.

* * * * *

"We have to go to him," Lenora insisted, her eyes pleading.

"I sense it too," Kaiya chimed in, jumping to her feet. "The western edge of the forest."

The Na'zoran general stood and barked commands to his troops. "To your mounts! Make ready to charge!"

The Na'zorans ran to their horses, dodging the elves who had been listening nearby. Hearing there was trouble, the elves scattered, some of them racing for cover, others racing for their weapons.

Lenora started to run toward the forest, but River blocked her path. "You must stay," he said. "We will need your healing skills. I will find Rogin."

Lenora did not reply. She stood with her feet firmly rooted to the ground as she watched her life mate heading off through the forest.

Isandra raised her fingers to her lips and whistled loudly for her own regiment to assemble. Raising her sword high, she didn't wait for anyone to follow. She dashed off into the woods in search of her brother and the enemies he was facing.

The Na'zorans charged after her, their horses dodging the thick trees. Hooves thundered, shaking the ground and announcing their impending arrival. Aldryg raised his sword high over his head and then lowered it, ordering his men to charge the invaders. Though he had never observed such creatures before, he did not waiver in his courage. These were beasts of evil, and they had to be stopped.

Kaiya raced toward the fray but was quickly overtaken by the nimble, long-legged elves who ran alongside her. Mel rushed forward to her side.

"What spells work against these things?" he asked, breathing heavily. "I've never fought using magic."

"I don't know what earth mages do," she replied, still moving forward. "If you're not confident enough with magic then find a weapon."

Mel stopped in his tracks. Years ago, he had considered himself among the finest archers in his clan. But he hadn't handled a bow since becoming a shaman, and that was thirty years ago.

With no other choice, Mel scanned the area, spotting a fallen elf. Approaching the lifeless figure, a sword still clutched in his bloodied hand, Mel reached for the bow and quiver strapped to his back. "Let's hope I have better luck than you did," he said.

Running forward, Mel found a suitable tree that he could easily climb to a useful height. Standing four branches up, Mel took aim at a large spider that was thrashing its massive pincers at a pair of swordsmen. Knocking the arrow to the string, he focused on his target. Holding his breath, he released the arrow and followed its path as it sped toward the spider. The arrow embedded itself between the two largest of the spider's eight eyes.

Raising his eyebrows in surprise, he muttered to himself, "I guess I'm not as rusty as I thought."

Kaiya blasted a path between the enemies using energy attacks to fling them out of the way. A red-robed sorcerer focused on her location, sensing her immense power. Knowing her essence would make a fine prize for his master, the sorcerer turned his mount to intercept her.

Three tiger-striped beasts turned their attentions to the dwarf as well. They leapt with fearsome power, baring their fangs and readying their claws. Kaiya was prepared. She reached into her magic and threw out her hands, shielding herself from their attack. Each glanced off her energy shield, falling to the ground stunned. Before she could block again, the sorcerer unleashed a fireball that narrowly missed her, landing with great force at her feet. She stumbled, losing her balance and hitting the ground.

Mel caught sight of the fireball and Kaiya scrambling to her feet. Above was her attacker, readying another fire attack. An orange glow emitted from his hand, and he pulled it back to launch it. Mel reacted first, firing his arrow straight through the sorcerer's hand. Pulling on his mount's reins reflexively, the sorcerer sent the beast hurtling through the air, trying to regain its balance.

It was the opportunity Kaiya needed. Sending lightning from her fingertips, she blasted the beast, charring it. The rider tumbled to the ground, flailing his limbs as he fell. Striking the forest floor below, the sorcerer did not move again.

Kaiya glanced back to view the archer who had bought her the time she needed to defend herself. Spotting Mel perched high on a limb, she gave him a nod of thanks. Mel responded by firing off two more arrows, both of which found their targets in the hearts of wolfbeasts.

River moved slower than the others but found his way to the battle nonetheless. By taking the side path, he avoided the majority of the enemies and focused his own magic to finding his injured son. Though he was still not well, he pulled at the magic within himself, forcing it to guide him through the trees.

Stepping carefully among the roots and twisted vines, River moved closer to Rogin's lookout post. A feeling hit him hard, nearly doubling him over from its intensity. His son was near. Scanning the branches, River's eyes searched the leaves. Clinging to a wide branch was Rogin.

River did not hesitate. He reached into the water within the earth and projected his magic toward his son. Rogin floated down to his father's side, gently cradled on a bed of water. He was barely breathing, and his hand covered a deep puncture wound on his side where the wyvern's talons had pierced him.

Nearly exhausted from the spell he had cast, River knew he would have difficulty getting his son home. His senses weakened, he did not hear the blue-furred wolfbeast approaching. The snapping of a twig under its heavy foot caught River's attention, and he turned in time to see it leaping toward him. Raising an arm instinctively, he reached for his magic but found it too depleted to cast another spell.

There was no need. From behind a tree, Alyra jumped out, a small dagger in her hand. Without a hint of fear, she stepped between her father and the beast, burying her dagger in its midsection. She stared at the beast's black eyes as it yowled in pain. Swallowing hard, Alyra continued to stare at the creature as it crumpled to the ground.

River grabbed her arm and spun her around. "You shouldn't be here!" he shouted. The wolfbeast flailed, attempting to sit up and continue the fight. River grabbed a fallen limb and brought it down hard on the creature's head. "Go back to the village, Alyra!" he shouted.

"You need my help!" she replied defiantly. Grabbing at her brother's feet, she attempted to drag him away from danger.

River placed a hand softly on his daughter's arm. "I will carry him," he said. Stooping low, he mustered his remaining strength to sling the injured elf over his shoulder. "Let's go," he said. Struggling under his son's weight, he slowly made his way back toward the village, his young daughter leading the way.

The battle continued to rage behind them, with Isandra wildly swinging her sword at the invaders. Kaiya fought her way to the elf warrior's side, continuing to summon energy from the air.

"Can't you hit them all with lightning?" Isandra called over the noise.

"There are too many of our own soldiers in the way," Kaiya replied, blasting at a massive spider.

Mel hopped down from his tree and rolled across the forest floor to stand beside the dwarf. "More are headed this way," he said. "I saw them from the treetops. At least a hundred foot soldiers. Probably more."

"Call to the forest," Kaiya said.

Mel didn't understand. Wrinkling his brow, he waited for an explanation.

"I can't do this," the dwarf said. "You must."

Still not knowing quite what she wanted, Mel let out a deep breath. Closing his eyes, he focused his energy into the earth, grasping at the magic inside. *Drive them away,* he commanded with his thoughts. It was the same technique he used when commanding a tree to heal or grow strong. He wasn't sure if it would work, but he had to try something. Reaching deeper into the earth, he commanded it again. *Drive these enemies away.*

A rumble sounded from deep in the earth, and the ground quaked beneath them, knocking most of the beasts and elves off balance. Branches and leaves began to move, swaying and rocking. The dryads released themselves from their havens inside the trees and joined their allies to defend the forest.

Hundreds of dryads emerged, projecting a bright green light in their outstretched hands. Focusing the beam at the invaders, they blinded the twisted creatures, driving them away from the elves. Stumbling and falling, the creatures hurried to escape the attacking dryads, retreating westward to the ships that had carried them to this land.

General Aldryg didn't waste a moment. Summoning his troops to his side, they reformed the charge and set off after the attackers. Colliding with the backs of the retreating beasts, the horses crushed them beneath their hooves and continued running.

Ahead were the soldiers Mel had seen. They would not be spared.

Only a few of them managed to make it back to the ship. Running as fast as she could, Kaiya emerged into the clearing in time to see the Na'zorans celebrating and the ship pulling away from the shore. Rushing to the water's edge, Kaiya summoned her energy and called upon the heavens. From high above, a wide bolt of lightning split the sky directly above the ship. Bringing the bolt down on its hull, it burst into splinters, sending all of its passengers into the water below.

Turning away from the destruction, Kaiya felt the cold stare of eyes watching her from afar. Ulda's malice cut through her, chilling her to the bone. Defiantly she held her head up and projected a message back to him with her mind: *You're next.*

Chapter 17

With a heavy swipe of his hand, Ulda knocked the orb from its stand. His soldiers had been defeated by those disgusting elves and their Na'zoran pets. Only his own presence could have prevented the loss. Burning with frustration, the sorcerer regretted not having traveled to the Vale. The wizards he had sent in his place had proved themselves incompetent. His opportunity to bind the essences of the most powerful elves in the world had been lost.

Now what would he do? Without those souls, he might not have the power to defend himself from the counterattack that would surely follow. The elves and Na'zorans were working together, and that didn't fit into Ulda's plan. He intended to take each land individually, marching on them in turn with his full strength. Instead, he would have to wait for them to come to him. He must be ready.

Retrieving the glowing orb from the floor, Ulda cradled it momentarily in his hand. Kaiya's eyes stared back at him, issuing a challenge. Smirking, he placed the orb back on its base. What could one dwarf possibly do to him? True she was powerful, but he would have her in his collection sooner or later. She was no match for him, and she was certainly aware of it. Ulda gave her credit for her bravery, but she had no idea what she was up against. A quiet laugh escaped his throat as he turned away from the orb.

Focusing his attention to the pile of scrolls on his desk, he searched for the one recounting the details of his most recent research. Finding it, he clutched it in his hand and squeezed it to his chest. *This will keep the balance,* he thought. *It is nearly ready.* With both water and wind combined, he knew the elf-dwarf pair might pose a threat to him. River was weak, but he could recover, especially if he made the trek over the ocean.

Ulda's failure to capture River's mate had left him determined. Had River lost her, his mind would be too clouded to lead the armies against Ral'nassa. The matter was now more complicated than Ulda had anticipated. Finalizing his darkest research would have to take top priority. Once his new enchantment was ready, he would render his army invincible, and no one would be able to break the line. Ulda's ultimate success would be assured.

* * * * *

Prin raised his hand near his forehead to shield his eyes from the sun. A dark figure approached, moving fast upon the wind. As it came into view, he recognized the shining violet scales of a wyvern, a dark-clad figure sitting upon its back. Holding his breath, the servant realized what had happened. A single survivor had escaped the battle in the Vale. Where the others had either fallen or fled, this one returned home to his master.

Prin hurried away from the coast, making his way to the breeding pits. In the days since learning of his defeat, Ulda had stepped up production of his creatures to prepare for the impending storm. Though he had expected the majority of those who had gone to the Vale to return, that simply wasn't to be. The elves harbored a deadly secret—a sorceress who had mastered air. Her strength, combined with the skill of the elves, had proved too much for Ulda's minions.

For days Ulda had dwelt on the image of the woman in his orb. At first he had dismissed her, but he soon blamed her entirely for his defeat. Prin would stand silently by and watch as his master became obsessed with revenge. This dwarf, he claimed, had cost him what he wanted most: elven souls to add to his collection. Ulda still harbored a deep resentment of River, but his defeat at the hands of a woman, not to mention a dwarf woman, was more than he could take. Drunk with his desire for revenge, Ulda had not left his laboratory since. Prin expected his master would either finalize his secret plans or kill himself in the process.

Only moments after arriving at the pits, the wyvern and its rider touched down. Clearly exhausted, the sorcerer stepped off his mount and slowly approached the wyvern cage. Struggling with the latch, he opened the door, allowing his savior to step inside. Immediately, the beast devoured a pile of meat left behind by the other creatures in the pen. The pair had embarked on a long journey over open sea with no time to stop for nourishment.

Prin approached the sorcerer as he secured the cage door. The man had dark circles beneath his eyes and a pallid complexion. His robe was covered in dirt and the remnants of greenery from the forest. Though he was weary, he attempted to stand tall as the servant approached.

A rain barrel stood nearby, and Prin grabbed the metal cup that floated at its surface. Filling it with water, he passed it to the sorcerer. "I'm surprised to see you," he said.

"I must speak with Master Ulda," the man said after taking a long drink.

"I don't think that's wise," Prin cautioned. "He's quite angry with all of you. It might have been best if you'd chosen not to return."

"I am a loyal servant," the sorcerer replied. "I must give my master a full account of what occurred."

"He's already aware," Prin replied. "He observed the entire battle in his orb."

"The shaman?"

Prin stared at the sorcerer blankly. He had heard nothing of a shaman, only Ulda's ramblings about the dwarf. "What shaman?" he asked.

"The one who woke the dryads," the sorcerer replied. "I've never seen anything like it."

"Did you miss the destruction of the ship?" Prin asked. "Were you not driven away by the air sorceress?"

The robed man shook his head. "The earth wizard was far more powerful."

"Impossible," Prin replied, despite his uncertainty. Ulda had clearly sensed the power of the dwarf, and her battle skills had drawn most of his attention. Had he observed the actions of an earth wizard, he had not informed Prin.

"I must see Master Ulda," the sorcerer insisted.

Prin shook his head, deciding not to argue further. Spinning on a heel, he led the weary traveler across the yard and inside the tower where Ulda was hard at work on his plans.

"He might refuse to see you," Prin cautioned. "He's a busy man."

"The information I carry is vital," he said. "You must convince him."

Prin dismissed the words and continued ascending the spiral staircase. The sorcerer grabbed his arm, nearly knocking him off his balance. Grasping at the handrail, he barely stopped himself from falling. "What do you—" he started to say.

Staring intently into Prin's eyes, the sorcerer said, "It is imperative you convince him to speak with me," he said. "His life depends upon it."

"I'll do what I can," Prin replied, his tone annoyed. Being grabbed by the arm was not to his liking. He was beginning to hope Ulda would teach this man a lesson.

The sorcerer released Prin's arm. "Our master is in great danger," he said in a softer tone. "You of all people should want him safe."

Prin eyed the man suspiciously. It was possible he really did have important information. However, that would not quell Ulda's anger upon seeing one of his disgraced sorcerers. As far as Ulda was concerned, all of those who had been sent to the Vale were dead. He had no intention of launching a rescue. They had failed him, and that was the end of it.

The two men continued up the steps, finally arriving at the landing in front of Ulda's laboratory. Prin hesitated, his hand poised over the door. Glancing at his companion, he finally gave a swift knock. No voice sounded from the other side. After a moment's wait, Prin knocked again and pushed the door open a tiny bit.

"Master?" Prin called inside.

"Can't this wait?" Ulda shouted back. He stood with his shoulders stooped, poring over his work. The edges of his robe were creased, as if he had repeatedly crumpled it in his hands.

"Forgive me, Master," Prin said. "I have someone here who wishes to see you. He says it's a matter of some urgency."

"Who is it?" Ulda asked, his patience already gone.

Prin realized he did not know the name of the sorcerer who was standing next to him.

"It's Varl," the sorcerer called inside.

"Impossible," Ulda huffed. "He's dead." He did not look up from his scrolls.

"No, Master," Varl said. "I survived the battle. I've come bearing news you must hear." Boldly, the sorcerer stepped inside, pushing his way past Prin.

Prin followed him inside, maintaining a safe distance for fear of Ulda's wrath. He had no desire to be struck by whatever might come flying in Varl's direction, magic or otherwise.

"Master?" Varl said.

A low growl sounded in Ulda's throat. Why did they insist on interrupting his work? Could they not see he was not interested in their company or conversation? Spinning around, he shouted, "Fool! How dare you flee from the battle? You were to stand your ground!" With heavy steps, he marched toward Varl, his dark eyes piercing the sorcerer's soul.

"I beg your forgiveness," Varl said, falling to his knees. "There was no more I could do, and I knew someone must make it back to warn you."

Ulda threw his hands up in frustration. "I witnessed the battle. Your words are not necessary. Go!"

Varl stood back up, pleading with his master. "Master, please hear me out. There are things you did not see."

Ulda narrowed his eyes as he looked upon the sorcerer. "You doubt my abilities?" he asked, his voice low and quiet.

"No, Master," Varl replied. "The dwarf caught your eye, as well she should. But there was another, an earth mage."

"I sensed nothing of the kind," Ulda replied, waving his hand. Had there been another master wizard, Ulda would have easily sensed him. No living creature with power of any consequence was immune to his keen senses. Turning his back to the sorcerer, he headed back to his desk.

"Master, it was a Wild Elf," Varl continued, hoping Ulda was still listening. "He is a shaman. He summoned the dryads."

"That's very amusing," Ulda replied. "But you're wasting my time. Can't you see I have work to do?"

"Master, they are uniting the elements," Varl said, his voice passionate. "It is their ploy to defeat you."

Ulda looked up and stared out the window toward the sea. Unite the elements? Would that truly pose a threat to him? The thought sent a wave of uncertainty through his mind, and the hair stood on the back of his neck.

"It is the water elemental's plan," Varl continued. "I'm certain of it. He thinks that the combined elements can destroy you. Why else would two strangers be present in the Vale at this time?"

"Perhaps they are friends of his and nothing more," Prin offered, seeing that his master was becoming anxious.

"Normally," Ulda began, "I would kill you for deserting your post." Spinning around, he looked at Varl, who bowed his head. "This information is useful to me, so I shall allow you to remain alive." Taking a few steps toward Varl, Ulda asked, "How many elven souls did you bring me?"

Varl swallowed hard before replying, "None, Master. I failed you."

Ulda slowly shook his head and pressed his tongue to the back of his teeth. Looking at Prin, he said, "I should have sent you. Though you have few magical skills, you are at least loyal."

Prin inclined his head slightly in appreciation. "It is an honor to serve you."

Taking in a deep breath, Ulda let out an audible puff of air. "This earth mage of yours," he said. "He was too insignificant to draw my attention. What makes you think he has some hidden power?" The idea of uniting the elements had merit, but River was not a true elemental, nor were his friends. Four true elementals would certainly pose worthy opponents, but one hybrid elf and two master wizards were nothing to him.

"I did not sense any magic in him myself," Varl stated. "Though my powers of perception are far below yours, I am normally aware of any wizard in my vicinity. From him I sensed nothing. His power must be deeply rooted to be so well hidden."

Ulda placed his hand against his chin and rubbed it nervously. The power emanating from the dwarf had been almost overwhelming. He couldn't help but look her direction. Perhaps she had shielded the shaman's abilities from Ulda's gaze.

Approaching his orb once more, Ulda peered inside, willing it to show him the events happening in the Vale. Focusing his mind to the shaman, he brought Mel into view. His appearance was less intimidating than the dwarf. The elf was slight of build with no particular fire in his eyes. Ulda did sense magic from him, but it was no more significant than any other wizard. In his opinion, the shaman couldn't possibly be a master of earth magic. The power Ulda sensed was far too weak.

"Have you ever studied earth magic?" Ulda asked.

"Only as a young student," Varl replied. "I did not have much talent for it."

"I have mastered it," Ulda stated. "It's simpler than the others. You grab some magic from the ground and draw it through yourself. It provides little satisfaction." The sorcerer spoke more to himself than anyone else. If Varl was correct, how could this elf pose any sort of threat? "What other spells did you see him cast?" Ulda asked.

"None, Master," Varl replied. "I glimpsed him shooting a bow before he summoned the dryads. After that, I saw very little."

Ulda sighed. "An archer," he said, shaking his head. The image of Mel disappeared from the orb. "This man is nothing to me," he said. As the words escaped his mouth, he remembered something from his training centuries ago. There are those so attuned to the earth that their magic is nearly imperceptible, even to the mightiest sorcerer. These earth wizards gave no outward signs of magic until they cast a spell. At that time, they could call upon powers seated deep in the ancient foundations of the world. Ulda felt himself shiver. Could River have found such a person and recruited him to his army?

Prin sensed the heaviness in the air brought on by Ulda's shifting mood. Glancing over at Varl, he suspected the sorcerer could feel it too.

"Leave me," Ulda commanded. The two men did not hesitate this time.

Leaning against his desk, Ulda considered the possibility of River and the others standing against him. They had water, earth, and air. All they lacked was fire. Did they intend to travel to the Red Isle and recruit a true fire elemental? Ulda dismissed the idea. It would be far too tedious, and elementals would not be easily convinced. River had nothing to offer it.

Scanning his memory, Ulda's mind turned to thoughts of Telorithan, who lived less than a day's travel from the Vale. True he had worshipped the man as a child. In every way, Ulda desired to be like Telorithan. It wasn't until he had nearly completed his training to become a master wizard that he realized he could exceed everything Telorithan had ever accomplished. He still admired and respected the sorcerer, but he had no need to imitate him. Ulda was already far more powerful than his former idol.

Ulda ran down the list of what he might be facing should an invasion end up on his doorstep. River was weak without the Spirit, of that much he was certain. Should he venture to the ocean, he would become stronger, but he would never again possess the strength he once held. The air mage was nothing but a dwarf. Ulda was convinced he could defeat her easily if given the chance. The shaman's power barely registered, and earth magic took a long time to induce, so Ulda felt certain that he could defeat the elf as well. That left only Telorithan, should River manage to bring him to his side. He could pose a significant threat, since he still possessed an elemental within him. Confident in his own abilities, Ulda yearned for the chance to face the infamous wizard. What better way to prove himself once and for all?

Taking a deep breath and letting it out slowly, Ulda attempted to refocus on his work. The answer was so near he could almost grasp it. If he could unlock the secret of his masterwork in time, no army could hope to stand against his own. Now, more than ever, he needed to complete his research.

Chapter 18

Alyra threw open the door of the wide silver tree
that served as the House of Medicine. Inside, Lenora
had already made preparations to receive the
wounded. She and the other healers of the village
stood inside, awaiting the arrival of wounded soldiers.

"I have him," River announced as he stepped
through the door, his son still slung over his shoulder.

"Bring him here," Lenora said, approaching one of
the cots. Near the bed she had placed several vials of
liquid and bundles of herbs.

Rogin groaned slightly as his father placed him on
the cot as gently as possible. His skin was pale, and he
had lost a frightening amount of blood in his
encounter with the wyvern. Lenora immediately
examined her son, checking his pulse and breathing

patterns while River held pressure against the wound. Alyra stood to the side, her eyes wide, fearing that her brother was slowly slipping away.

"Can you heal him?" the girl asked, her voice barely more than a whisper.

Placing her right hand over her son's heart and her left upon the puncture in his side, Lenora spread white magic throughout his body. Focusing on the wound, she cleansed it with magic and sealed it to stop the bleeding. "He will need time to heal, but he will survive," she announced, the tension draining from her voice.

River squeezed his son's hand and looked at his life mate. "You must save your strength," he said. "There may be many wounded to treat."

Lenora nodded slowly. She knew well she couldn't use magic for all her patients. It took a great deal of power to cast healing spells of such potency, and she would exhaust her supply and herself, rendering her too fatigued to work. She had to save her strength if she was going to tend the injured.

Releasing his son's hand, River said softly, "It is time I gathered the final member of my party. We mustn't delay our march against Ulda."

With her eyes closed, Lenora drew in a deep breath. "Be careful," she managed to say. It was the only advice she could give. The man he was about to encounter was dangerous, and River was still weak. Knowing how powerful his two companions were, Lenora hoped they would be able to stand against Telorithan should things go awry.

To Alyra, River gave a stern look. "You must stay here and help your mother. Do not follow me, and do not sneak away."

River was rarely strict with the girl, and she felt the seriousness of his demand. Quickly nodding her head, she agreed. This was one time she would choose to obey.

River stepped outside the House of Medicine as a wave of injured elves and Na'zorans were carried his direction. There were many more than he expected. Standing aside, he allowed those who bore the injured to pass by him. There was nothing he could do to help. Lenora was the best healer in the Vale, and she would give them their best chance for survival. River briefly wondered how many might lay dead in the woods, but he pushed the thought aside. He had to focus on the task ahead.

To his relief, he spied Mel and Kaiya together coming out of the tree line. Both appeared unharmed. If anything, they appeared to have been rejuvenated by the battle. Mel stared at the bow in his hands, marveling at its construction, until River caught his attention.

"It's time," River said as he approached.

"For what?" Mel asked.

Kaiya rolled her eyes and shook her head. "To join with the fourth element," she explained. "You don't think very far ahead, do you?"

Mel shrugged. "I'm kind of figuring things out as I go," he said. Looking down at the bow once more, he still couldn't believe he had been able to use it. At least his years of training hadn't gone to waste. "I think I'll hang on to this," he said. "Just in case."

"Don't bring it along to meet Telorithan," River requested. "He is immune to those weapons, but he will see it as an insult nonetheless."

"I'm ready to leave," Kaiya stated. The others nodded in agreement. Together the three made their way across the village and down the sloping hill to the riverbank. The sight of clean water brought tears to River's eyes.

"You two did this," he said, his breath escaping. "I did not have the strength. My people thank you."

Kaiya reached up to pat his back. "It was our pleasure," she replied, glancing at Mel.

River held his hand above the water and summoned a small amount of magic. The spell was simple—one he had performed hundreds of times with little effort. Though it took more power than usual, he was able to raise a raft from the depths.

"Not bad," Mel said, attempting to encourage his ailing friend.

Kaiya shot him a sideways glance. *Men are so tactless,* she projected with her mind.

Mel startled slightly at the sound of her voice in his head. With a sigh, he ignored her words.

The trio climbed aboard the raft and sat comfortably as it floated along the current. There were no fish to speak of, but dragonflies had returned to buzz the top of the water. As they continued farther downstream, the water once again became murky.

"I guess our spell couldn't reach this far," Mel commented.

"At least the water is safe in the Vale," River said. "I doubt anyone could cleanse the entire river with Ulda still living."

"That brings up another question," Mel said. "Are we going to kill him, trap his essence, or what?"

River stared off into the distance. "He must be destroyed."

Kaiya peered down into the murky water and bravely stuck in a hand. "It's not poisonous here," she commented. "It's just filthy." Sniffing at her fingers, she regretted having touched the water.

"The poison had one purpose," River replied. "It was not needed away from the Vale."

Kaiya understood. The Spirit had been Ulda's target, and this remaining filth was just an aftereffect. Sensing a great feeling of loss emanating from River, she closed her mind to his pain to avoid being overwhelmed. "We will make this right," she said sincerely.

Silently they floated, seemingly for hours, as the weather became colder from winter's chill. No birds were around, and a large section of forest had been cleared back, creating a path through the woods to a tall stone tower standing in the distance.

"Amazing," Mel said, pointing to a section of water near the bank. A portion of the river had been cleared and was teeming with life, while all around it flowed the murky water of Ulda's curse.

"Even a fire elemental needs water," Kaiya said, chuckling.

"Yes," River replied. "Telorithan has need of the same nourishment as anyone else."

"He cleared this section alone?" Mel asked out loud. It had taken both him and Kaiya together to clear the section near the Vale, and there were still no living fish. Somehow, Telorithan had managed alone what they could not achieve together.

"He has had more years to perfect his art than both of you together," River explained. Willing the raft to obey him, he moved it to the bank where the three companions could step up onto dry land. As they stepped away, the raft sank into the depths.

Mel's brow wrinkled with worry as he watched the raft slip away.

"I will have the strength to raise it again," River said with a faint trace of a smile on his lips.

"Is everyone reading my mind today?" Mel asked, agitated. "It's getting a little old."

River and Kaiya exchanged glances. "It's part of our nature," Kaiya said. "Forgive us. We'll be more guarded in the future."

The path beneath their feet remained green, but all around them were signs of winter. Obviously,

Telorithan preferred the warmth of summer that graced his native land rather than the ever-changing climate he had come to live in. Despite traces of snow on the trees around them, the travelers stayed relatively warm.

It was a few miles' walk to the tower, and Mel enjoyed the duality of seasons around him. It was a trick he decided he must learn. If Kaiya and Telorithan were both capable of it, then he should be too. It could only help his people and the forest around them to be able to extend the growing season when necessary. He would not abuse the spell though. A period of winter was necessary for many of the plants to thrive. The cycle of death and rebirth must not be eliminated entirely as it seemed to be here in Telorithan's territory.

Only steps away from the tower, they were greeted by a bright flash of red-orange light. Upon the balcony of his spire, Telorithan stood above the travelers, his stark white hair riding gently on the breeze. Despite his advanced age, he appeared to be in his prime, with no lines or traces of a hard-lived life upon his face. His eyes a piercing blue, he gazed down upon his guests, a smirk gracing his lips.

"River, I see you've kept your promise to visit me," Telorithan said. "And you've brought friends."

"I have," River replied, peering up at the sorcerer. "It is time you released the fire elemental."

Telorithan laughed. "I'm afraid I must decline."

"You've grown too comfortable," River stated. "Lorith is waning."

The sorcerer's demeanor changed, becoming more defensive. Straightening his back, the smile faded from his lips. His gaze pierced through Mel, causing the elf to shudder. Next, he looked at Kaiya, but found he could not penetrate her thoughts. Immediately, he knew she was the one who had defeated him in battle hundreds of years ago, when he had attempted to bind River's essence. "You keep poor company, River," he stated with disgust. "This one would have been eliminated long ago if I had the energy to spare on revenge."

Kaiya stepped forward, but River blocked her path with his hand. With his eyes, he beseeched her to ignore the comment. It was best to try appealing to his ego rather than risk a confrontation.

"You will come with me," River said. "The power that has taken Ral'nassa threatens us all. We need your help."

"You cannot command me to go anywhere," Telorithan replied. "Your master is dead, and you lack the strength to coerce me."

Kaiya, unable to hold back any longer, stepped forward. "I bested you once, and I'll do it again!" she shouted, raising her hands to strike.

The sorcerer only laughed at her. "You can handle this problem on your own. Go and leave me in peace before I run out of patience."

"Let's go," Kaiya said. "We don't need this coward."

"Master Ulda cannot be defeated without fire," River reminded her. Turning back to the sorcerer, he said, "Lorith, you know we cannot do this without you. Help us."

At the repeated mention of his birth name, the sorcerer cringed. He had taken on the longer form when he became convinced he could bind the soul of a god. It was best to be named properly if one expected to become godlike. Lorith was the name given to him by his parents, who were too weak to defend themselves when the Grand Council had crushed their rebellion. It shamed him to be called by it.

"He won't do it because he's too scared," Kaiya said. "Forget him." She turned as if to walk away.

"Perhaps you'd like to prove you're as powerful as you say," Telorithan called to her. "You seem eager to prove your skill, but I warn you. I have not been idle all these years. You might find me a more challenging opponent than before."

"I have nothing to prove to you, coward," she replied hotly. "I beat you once, and you still have the scars to show for it. You're just hiding them behind one of your 'aren't I pretty' enchantments."

"Lorith," River called, "we need you. I know you're still in there somewhere. Fire has consumed you, but you have not gone away entirely. This is your chance to be free. No longer will you live in the elemental's grasp. Now you must control it, as it has controlled you for so long." River knew the truth behind what Telorithan had done. Instead of binding the elemental to him, he had been overwhelmed by it—losing himself in the process. The two had been locked in internal combat, the elemental constantly besting the sorcerer. "Please help us," River continued. "Put your torment to an end." Closing his eyes, he projected a burst of blue light that hung in the air before Telorithan's face.

261

Several moments of silence passed as Telorithan contemplated River's words, the blue light illuminating his tormented expression. "I am tired," the sorcerer whispered to himself.

Sensing the elf's inner struggle, River spoke again. "You are not immune to Ulda's evil," he said. "In time, you will fall to his power as well. The only way to stop him is to join us."

Turning his thoughts to the sea, Telorithan stretched his mind to the shores of Ral'nassa. He had been aware of Ulda's existence for some time, and he knew the elf wielded great power—possibly greater than his own. But so far, he had remained untouched by Ulda's schemes. After all, Telorithan was aware the sorcerer had learned from his own writings. In a way, Ulda was a protégé of Telorithan. Now, it seemed, the student had surpassed the master. Telorithan had never dreamed of mastering a fifth element. All he had craved was the strength of Yelaurad, the fire god.

Born on the Sunswept Isles, Telorithan had long exceeded the lifespan of an Enlightened Elf. His body was beginning to age, despite his spells to make himself appear younger. The presence of the elemental within him had taken its toll, and he had grown weary of the constant struggle. One last fight to prove he could best the greatest living sorcerer was just what he needed.

"It is time," the sorcerer said. In a flash of red-orange light, he appeared on the ground next to his visitors. "I will go with you."

Chapter 19

Standing at the forest's edge, Lenora gave thanks to the Goddess. Her son's life had been spared, and he was now recovering in the House of Medicine. Through her efforts, he had regained consciousness and spoken to his mother, filling her heart with great joy. Praising the Goddess for her mercy and kindness, Lenora offered a prayer of thanks that few lives had been lost. Only six elven lives and two Na'zorans had been lost to Ulda's invasion force. However, one was too many, and Lenora wished she could spare their families the grieving they would have to endure.

She stood motionless, her head bowed in reverence, as the bodies of the fallen were lifted and carried past her. *May these souls find peace in the world to come*, she whispered to the earth. The footfalls of the bearers moved silently through the forest, carrying home the elves who would wake no more. Lenora wept for her brothers and sisters. Though death only brought a release of the spirit into the next realm, it was painful to lose them in such a way. They should have had many years ahead of them. Knowing they had died to save those who could not fight—the children and the elderly—was of little comfort. Each loss was a heavy blow to her heart.

Fluttering in a nearby tree caught Lenora's attention, and she broke from her meditative state. A silver-skinned dryad emerged from her tree, taking careful steps over the grass to speak with Lenora.

"A somber day," the dryad said.

"Indeed," Lenora agreed, her throat slightly raspy. "You're Dela, right?" The dryad was familiar to her, but not one she had ever known well.

"I am," Dela replied. "I have come to tell you that my sisters and I will not sleep again until the evil that threatens this land is destroyed. Your shaman has awakened us, even those of us who have slept for many long years."

Lenora had studied with the dryads in her youth, but as the centuries passed, there were fewer and fewer of the tree guardians awake in the forest. It was a sad loss, but one that Lenora had come to accept. The dryads had shaped the forests for millennia and had looked after its well-being since time began. They were eternal and had earned a period of rest.

"Your help is most appreciated," Lenora replied, managing a weak smile. The heaviness she felt inside would not allow more than that.

"Go in peace, Sister," the dryad said. "No more harm will come to your people."

Lenora nodded her head and turned to face her village. The dryads could do only so much. With the armies preparing to march for Ral'nassa, Lenora knew that harm would likely come to many of those who faced battle. The dryads could protect only the forested side of the Vale, not those who would be leaving it.

Moving back through the village, Lenora noticed her daughter pointing and shouting orders to the troops who would soon depart for war. Isandra carried herself with such dignity and strength, Lenora could not help but be proud. Though she had chosen a more difficult route than her mother, Isandra was a brave soul and worthy of great respect. Lenora wished only for the safe return of her beloved child.

Approaching her daughter, Lenora said, "How soon will you be leaving?"

"I want to be ready when Father returns," Isandra stated, her eyes still locked on the troops who were filing into formation.

Lenora looked away, wringing her hands. So many had gathered, which meant few would be left to guard the Vale. Even with the dryads protecting her home, Lenora felt uneasy. She knew she had no skills for battle, but those under her care would need protection. With luck, many of the injured soldiers would be back on their feet before trouble could find them again.

"How is Rogin?" Isandra asked, startling Lenora out of her worrying.

"He's better," she replied. "I expect he'll be up and around in a matter of days."

"That's good to hear," Isandra replied. "I'm sorry he won't be able to come with us. He will be missed."

Lenora looked over the regiments that stood before her daughter. "It looks like they're more than willing to follow your lead in his stead."

Isandra nodded. "They are brave warriors. They will fight to avenge their fallen comrades."

"Thirsting for vengeance will only lead them to ruin," Lenora cautioned. "Have them fight instead for the safety of the families they leave behind."

Dipping her head, Isandra acknowledged the wisdom in her mother's words.

"How go your preparations?" Aldryg asked as he made his way to the women.

"We are nearly ready," Isandra replied. "Shall we prepare the bodies of your fallen to be returned to Na'zora?"

Shaking his head, the general replied, "No. Leave them to the forest. It is as beautiful a place as any to rest."

"No harm will ever come to them again," Lenora said softly.

"How are your patients?" he inquired.

"Healing well," she replied. "We are fortunate more were not lost."

"There may be more death yet to come in this battle," Aldryg said.

"Nevertheless, we must go," Isandra stated, looking at her mother.

Lenora offered no argument. She knew it was imperative that Ulda be stopped, but it pained her to see the faces of her kinsmen who might not be returning. With her own daughter and life mate among the troops, she could do little more than pray to the Forest Goddess for their safety.

At the edge of her vision, Lenora spied River returning to the village. At his side strode Kaiya, an expression of satisfaction on her face. Mel walked a few steps behind them, his demeanor casual, as always. What she saw next sent a chill down her spine. Slowly following behind the others was Telorithan, his mere presence bringing a darkness to the Vale that left Lenora feeling unsettled. The white-haired sorcerer kept a distance between himself and the others, his eyes scanning the area as if he were hatching a plan. Lenora did not trust him.

Telorithan ignored her gaze, as well as ignoring the rest of the elves in the village. Keeping only himself as company, he leaned lazily against the trunk of a wide silver tree and crossed his arms, his expression one of boredom.

River approached Lenora, his features softening as he came closer to her. Her face showed concern as she continually glanced over at the sorcerer.

"Let him be," River said. "He will not harm anyone here."

Kaiya couldn't contain a laugh. "Not with me around anyway."

River turned to look at his companion. "I would ask you not to provoke him," he said. "If he is angered, he might change his mind about helping us. There is a duality to him, and those two sides do not always agree. We need his help, and we will have it as long as we are careful when speaking to him."

Kaiya smirked but kept quiet. She had spoken her piece already, and she had little left to say to the sorcerer. Out of respect for River, she would cease her jibes at Telorithan's expense. Ridding the world of Ulda was far more important. If that meant working with her enemy, she would do it.

"How fares our son and the others who were injured?" River asked.

"Much better than before," Lenora replied. "We've lost no more lives, and our son will recover."

"That is good to hear," he said. "We must leave soon, and Rogin will be needed to protect this land."

"I'm not sure he'll be in fighting shape so quickly," Lenora stated.

"Whether he's back on his feet in a day or a month, he will always be needed to protect the Vale," River replied.

"The dryads will continue to look over this place while we're gone," Mel added, hoping to ease Lenora's fears. "The Vale won't be left unprotected."

"He's right," Kaiya agreed. "And anything approaching from the east will run into us." She was well aware that River's spells of protection had fallen when the Spirit died. There was no magic to protect the Vale on its eastern border. "I can lay down a few spells before I leave as well."

"That's much appreciated," Lenora said with a half-smile. "It will bring some comfort to those who are staying behind." Looking around, it seemed as if the vast majority of elves would be marching off to battle. Few were staying behind who were capable of providing any defense.

"Maybe you should see if Telorithan wants to put down some protection spells too," Mel suggested with a grin.

Kaiya pursed her lips and remained silent.

"It's best to leave him alone," River replied.

Mel shrugged, wondering why no one had a sense of humor about the situation. It was better to laugh than fall apart worrying.

"The army is nearly ready," River said. Taking Lenora's hand, he asked, "Would you talk with me a while before we depart?"

"Of course," she replied.

The pair walked away from the commotion in town, heading toward the riverbank just outside their home. A large weeping willow stood tall near the water, a silver bench sitting at its base. Here they had spent many long hours discussing various matters throughout their lives together. The sound of the waterfall drowned out the noise of the village, and it gave them the sense that they were the only two people left in the world.

Lenora sat next to her life mate and leaned her head against his chest. It pained her greatly to think of him leaving. Seldom had they been parted over the centuries.

River held her close and sighed. "I wish we could stay this way forever."

Those words troubled Lenora, who sensed he meant more than he was saying. He was still unwell, and she feared he would have a difficult time in his travels. "Perhaps I should come along to tend to your health while you march," she suggested.

"No, my love," he replied. "You must stay here and tend to Rogin and the others." After a pause, he added, "I am selfish and have no desire to be parted from you."

Puzzled, Lenora asked, "If you don't want to be parted, then why shouldn't I come along?" His statement made no sense.

Slowly, River said, "Having you along would complicate matters. Though I've cherished every moment of the last eight-hundred-and-forty years, I fear I will not be able to do what has to be done if you are beside me."

Lenora felt a cold chill on her spine. Lifting her head, she looked into her life mate's sapphire eyes. "What has to be done?" she asked, feeling a lump rise in her throat.

"There is a difficult decision to be made, and I would choose you above all things."

Feeling a heaviness enter her heart, Lenora began to understand his meaning. For the first time, she realized she may never see him again. This mission to end evil might well claim his life. As she tried to speak, she found herself stumbling on her words. Nothing seemed an appropriate response except for the tears that were streaming down her cheeks. Pressing her face into his chest, she allowed herself to grieve the loss that was yet to come.

For several minutes, they held each other in silence. Sensing that the moment of departure was near, River leaned in to kiss his life mate. Lenora welcomed his embrace, feeling the warmth of his lips against her own. If only she could hold him close to her forever.

Isandra approached, not bothering to hide the heaviness of her boots. The pair looked up at her, their faces showing acceptance.

"We are ready to march," she announced. "The rest of our army awaits us in Na'zora."

River stood, followed slowly by Lenora. She squeezed his hand and did her best to steady her breathing.

Isandra looked upon her mother with concern. "I will look after his well-being," she promised. "You need not fear."

Lenora bit her lip, forcing herself to remain silent about her fears. Wrapping her arms tightly around her daughter, she said, "Come back to me, child." As she stepped away, her eyes once again filled with tears.

"You have my word on it," Isandra replied with confidence.

The trio headed back into the village, where the majority of the army was mounted and ready to ride. The rest of the soldiers would travel on foot, spurred on by the magic of the forest until they reached Na'zora. Each elf would dedicate his own supply of magic, no matter how small, to giving speed to the army. Too much time had been lost already, and Ulda must not be allowed to ready his defense.

The Vale's remaining citizens gathered at the center of town to farewell the soldiers. Alyra stood among them, but moved to her mother's side as she spotted her returning.

Kneeling down next to his young daughter, River said, "Stay close to your mother, and help her when you can. You mustn't try to follow us. You are too young to encounter such evil, and there is much left to do in your lifetime." Clutching the girl next to his chest, his heart filled with both sadness and joy. Leaving her was a bittersweet moment. He must go to ensure she would have a future, but he hated the thought of leaving the child behind. There was so much she could learn from him, and it was uncertain whether he would be able to teach her.

Choking back her tears, Alyra could only nod. Hoping to show her father that she could indeed be strong, she refused to cry, though her heart was about to burst. Trying desperately to follow Isandra's example, she wanted to show courage rather than sorrow.

Choosing to walk rather than ride, Mel marched toward the river to provide crossing for the rest of the troops. Kneeling next to the bank, he reached into the earth and summoned a thicket of interwoven vines to bridge the water. Satisfied with his work, he turned to find Kaiya standing with her arms crossed.

"I see you've managed to impress yourself again," she said with a laugh.

Shaking his head, Mel did not respond. She slapped him on the back and strode at his side across the freshly constructed bridge. Waving to the others, she let them know it was safe to cross.

Telorithan chose a large black steed to carry him into battle. Riding outside the formation, he made his way across the bridge and stopped far away from the others. He had no intention of going near the humans, believing their kind to be lowly and uncivilized.

River gave Lenora a final kiss, and he lovingly patted the cheek of his youngest daughter. Taking one last look at his home among the silver trees, he mounted his horse and crossed the river. Looking down into its depths, he sensed the emptiness that still resided there, despite Kaiya and Mel's efforts to clean it. *Things will be made right,* he said to himself.

Lenora hugged Alyra to her side as she watched the soldiers depart. She lifted her hand, saying goodbye to those who might not return. In her mind, she repeated a single phrase: *Goddess watch over them.*

Chapter 20

A fresh layer of snow blanketed the Wildlands, leaving the world buried in a sea of white. The army marched on, their feet crunching on the ground beneath. Many of the elves sang songs as they went—songs that reminded them of simpler times. Not only did they sing epic songs that told tales of ages past, they sang simple melodies often learned in childhood. For the most part, the Na'zorans remained silent, listening to the music of the elves.

Watchful eyes peered out from the trees, offering blessings of the forest to the soldiers. Several trees shook their branches, discarding the snow that had gathered on their boughs. This brought smiles to the faces of the elves and wonder to the minds of the humans.

With the combination of elemental magic and the primal powers of the dryads, the soldiers' steps were hastened, moving them farther ahead than expected each day. The soldiers found their bodies energized and they rarely grew tired, allowing them to march on both day and night.

When at last they stopped for a rest, Isandra insisted they sleep in shifts, leaving two-thirds of the army awake while one-third slept. She believed this would provide enough resistance should anything attack in the night. General Aldryg did not argue. In the short time he had known her, he had come to trust the elf woman's judgment. She was more dedicated than any soldier he had ever met, and she knew this land better than him.

Kaiya fashioned a ring of rocks and drew heat from the air to light a fire. It roared to life with a silver blaze.

Mel sat down beside her. "Way to draw what was left of the warmth out of the air," he jibed.

Kaiya placed her hands in front of the fire. "Did you forget to put on your woolen underwear?" she asked, grinning.

"Yes, did you pack any extra?" he joked back. The pair laughed and enjoyed a rare moment of leisure.

With battle ahead, it was uncertain how many more moments like this would come.

Looking toward the edge of camp, Kaiya asked, "Why does Telorithan stay so far from us? He's ridden outside the group since we left the Vale, and I haven't heard him utter a single word."

"He considers all of us beneath him," River said as he approached. Taking a seat cross-legged on the ground, he added, "Lorith has always preferred solitude. It's best to leave him to it."

Kaiya looked again and saw a flash of red in the sorcerer's eyes. Her body tensed slightly, wondering if he might be planning to attack. Reaching toward his mind, she found it heavily guarded. To her relief, she sensed no magic emanating from the man and allowed herself to relax a little. She continued to watch as he turned his back to the soldiers, staring off into the wilderness.

River reached into the satchel he had removed from his horse and pulled out a bundle wrapped in a dark velvet cloth. As the cloth was removed, both Kaiya and Mel sensed the presence of power and turned their attention to their friend. Even Telorithan's gaze turned back to see what was happening, his blue eyes alight with red fire.

"I thought it best to give you these now," River said. He passed a large white gem to Kaiya and a green one to Mel.

Kaiya turned the stone over in her hand, marveling how its facets caught the light of her fire. "It's beautiful," she said.

Mel observed his as well. "What does this do?"

River lifted a larger blue stone from the bundle and held it to the light. "We will need these to defeat Ulda," he explained. "These stones will magnify our powers while draining his."

Kaiya nodded in understanding. "One must be incredibly disciplined to use these." She glanced over at Mel. To River, she asked, "Do you think we're at that level?" She already believed herself to be, though she had not used such a tool before. It was Mel's abilities that worried her. He'd had only thirty years to study his craft, while the others had been honing their skills for centuries.

"Yes," River said with confidence.

Mel suspected Kaiya's question had referred to him, but it did not bother him in the slightest. He was well aware of his lack of training. Most of what he knew he had learned on his own, though the dryads in his forest home had been eager to answer his many questions and show him a few of their spells.

Closing his hand around the gem, he felt the energy of the earth radiating through it. His body tingled at its touch, and he felt his mind yearning to open to the power of the stone. He resisted the urge, knowing it was not yet time to use it. Tucking it into the breast pocket of his elk-skin vest, he blocked the temptation from his mind.

"You see," River said with a smile. "It comes naturally to him. Earth mages are different from other elemental wizards."

Kaiya tilted her head and wondered if she should peak into Mel's thoughts. Did he realize the power he could draw with the gem's help? Probably not, she decided. Though she began to doubt when she saw a spark of green light in his eyes. Maybe he did realize it, and he was choosing not to experiment. *He's more disciplined than I thought. I'll have to start giving him more credit in the future.*

"You really should, you know," Mel responded with a grin.

Kaiya's mouth dropped open slightly, realizing he had just used her own trick against her. "I'm going to keep a closer eye on you from now on," she said, narrowing her eyes.

Mel burst out laughing and leaned his back against a tree. Helping him listen in on a smidgen of Kaiya's thoughts was only a tiny drop of what the gem could do, and he knew it. River had placed in his hands an object that could provide him with unfathomable power.

"Where did you get these?" Mel asked. He also wondered how much such an item would cost if purchased, and who was capable of crafting them.

"These were gifted to me," River replied. "The gems were crafted by the gods and given to the Guardian Elementals."

Mel leaned toward River and wrinkled his brow. "Guardian Elementals?"

"One guardian of each element was chosen by their respective gods. They have served to protect this world and banish the evil that threatened it."

"Well, I've got news for them," Mel replied. "There's plenty of evil in this world. It might not all be on Ulda's scale, but it's around." Apparently the guardians had fallen asleep or forgotten their duties.

River shook his head. "They do not interfere in the daily lives of Nōl'Deron's inhabitants. They protect the elements."

Mel swallowed, debating momentarily if he should ask the next question. "Why didn't they protect the Spirit in your river?"

River hung his head, his eyes focused on the gem in his hands. "There were none in the Vale at that time," he said.

Mel started to speak again, but a sharp glance from Kaiya made his tongue freeze to the roof of his mouth. She placed her hand on River's arm in an act of comfort, and Mel realized what had happened. At least, he thought he knew. He was well aware that the spirit of an elemental inhabited River's body. Could it have been the spirit of a Guardian that inhabited him? Was he limited by the elven body, and that's why he couldn't save the Spirit? Mel's mind swam, trying to imagine the possibilities.

River had been away in Na'zora at the time of the attack. Mel also recalled his first meeting with River, where he had sensed his power and mistaken him for the ancient God of Rivers, Mistonwey. If River possessed this gem at the time, perhaps Mel had sensed its godlike power. Shaking his head, Mel tried to put the thoughts away. They were too complicated, and he wasn't sure he was anywhere close to being on the right track.

Looking back at Kaiya, Mel realized he still didn't have her permission to speak. Instead, he stretched himself out by the fire and turned his gaze to the stars.

River unwrapped the final stone, its red glow piercing the night. It was warm to the touch despite the cold winter air surrounding it.

"Can we trust Telorithan to use that wisely?" Kaiya asked. "He did crave the power of a god, after all." She glanced over at the sorcerer, whose eyes had not left the trio since River produced the bundle with the gems.

"We must trust him," River replied. "There is no other way."

Kaiya wasn't sure she liked that response. She considered Ulda and Telorithan to be nearly equal in their levels of evil. Neither would do good had they the power of a god. With a sigh, she thought, *At least Telorithan would keep to himself as he's always done. Ulda brings his evil to torment the people around him.* With no other choice, she accepted River's decision.

River wrapped the cloth around the blue and red gems, and returned them to his bag. Tonight was not the right time to give Telorithan his gem. That would come later. The white-haired sorcerer turned his back on the trio once more and stared off into the night.

As River slept, Kaiya moved to his side. Placing her hands on his head, she spread silver magic throughout his body. Mel noticed her actions and sat up.

"What are you doing?" he asked, whispering.

"He still isn't well," she replied. "He needs help replenishing his magic until we reach the ocean."

Mel understood. Most elves could recover their supply with rest, but Mel had found it unnecessary. With his feet in connection to the earth, he never needed to worry about running low on magic. It never struck him as odd until now. He wasn't an elemental, though elementals replenished their magic by coming into contact with the element they represent. Kaiya was the same way. Mel didn't understand how it was possible, but he accepted his ability gratefully.

The following morning as they continued their snowy march, Mel decided it was time to ask the question he had been holding onto. Striding at River's side, he said, "I think it's time to tell me exactly what my role is in all this."

River looked at him questioningly.

"How are we going to stop Ulda?" Mel asked.

"Your part is to focus only on reaching into the earth and tapping its power," River replied. "You will do nothing to attack Ulda. Focus energy to your gemstone, and when the time is right, you will know what to do. I swear it. Please trust me."

Looking at the sincerity on River's face, Mel decided to drop the subject and trust his friend. His only regret was that he wouldn't be allowed to attack Ulda, the man responsible for the death of his beloved.

Kaiya scoffed. "Just tell him already," she said.

Mel's ears perked up. What was she talking about?

River replied, "He must figure things out for himself in his own time." Glancing at the dwarf, he added, "As you did."

Kaiya shrugged. "Fine, but he knows he's special, and someday he will be infinitely more powerful. He should also be aware he'll outlive everyone he's ever known."

Those words gave Mel something to contemplate. He had planned to join his lost love in the afterlife at some point. Now he was forced to wonder how long he would have to wait. Making a mental note, he planned to have a real talk with Kaiya once this was all over. She seemed far more willing to explain things than River.

A scene at the corner of his eye broke Mel away from his thoughts. Telorithan, who normally stayed at a distance, had moved closer to the trio. The sorcerer clutched an arm to his midsection, on his face a grimace of discomfort. Mel didn't know what to say. He looked over at Kaiya, who was staring wide-eyed, her eyebrows raised in surprise. Only River seemed to maintain his ever-calm demeanor. He rode over to Telorithan's side and placed a hand on the sorcerer's back.

"It will pass," River said.

Telorithan looked up at him, a hint of fear in his blue eyes. "Is this how you feel?" he asked.

River shook his head. "My duality is different from yours. I was gifted the spirit inside me. You took yours unnaturally."

Looking up, his face twisted in torment, he replied, "It was worth it." He managed to force a sideways smile. After a few more moments, he had composed himself, the pain in his abdomen subsiding.

River looked at him sincerely. "Lorith has been silent in this form far too long. He is ready to rest."

Telorithan stared at him but did not reply. Though his arrogance would not allow him to admit it, he had many regrets. His life had been a series of bad decisions—trapping an elemental among them. True it had provided him with immense power and abilities he could only dream of, but it had taken its toll on his mortal body. With each passing decade, he grew weaker, nearing his inevitable end.

* * * * *

Days in the snow finally gave way to clearer ground, but the air was no less frigid. Winter was not ready to relinquish its grasp on the land. The army moved at a quick pace, reaching the Na'zoran border in half the normal time. The elves were somewhat familiar with this form of magic, but the Na'zoran soldiers marveled at it. They had felt no difference in their speed. In fact, they believed themselves to be traveling at the usual pace, despite arriving at their homeland much faster than expected.

A scout sent by the king awaited the army's arrival and greeted them warmly at first sight. "Greetings," he called, recognizing General Aldryg. He ordered his own regiment to stay put, as these were not enemies arriving at the border. Riding out to meet them, he raised his hand in a gesture of peace. "Welcome to this land," he said, inclining his head to River. "You are most welcome."

Aldryg approached the scout and asked, "Is our army ready to march? The elves will lead us there in a day or less."

The scout appeared puzzled. "It is a two-day ride to the coast as you well know," he said.

Shaking his head, Aldryg replied, "Not with their combined magic it isn't."

Seeming to understand, the scout stated, "King Rykon has prepared the forces daily, in anticipation of your arrival. He will be ready to march the moment we arrive."

"Then let us not delay," Aldryg replied. Motioning for the troops to move forward, he took his place at the head of the line to lead them through Na'zora to the sea.

All across the land, citizens stepped outside to greet the soldiers. They lifted their voices in praise and good wishes, hoping that this army would indeed defeat the evil that had claimed the life of their beloved king.

As the army moved through the land, it was evident that the citizens were living in fear. The majority of the houses had been boarded up to prevent harm to the people inside should Ulda's forces attack. There were neither open markets nor signs of merchants along the roads. Commerce was already slow due to the winter conditions, but the looming threat of war had brought it to a grinding halt.

When at last they arrived in the palace district, King Rykon himself rode out to greet them. "Lord River," he began, "it is good of you to return." He embraced the elf before acknowledging the presence of Mel and Kaiya. Reaching out a hand to Mel, he said, "I am pleased to have you join us."

"You can thank River for that," Mel said.

Next, the king extended his hand to Kaiya. "My lady," he said respectfully.

Kaiya chuckled slightly. "Call me Kaiya, Your Majesty," she replied.

"My friends represent the elements," River stated. "Together we have a chance of defeating Ulda for good."

Rykon glanced around, immediately recognizing Telorithan. "You have strange friends, Lord River," he said in a hushed tone. "Are you sure you've chosen the wisest course of action?"

"I am," River replied.

Trusting in his father's good judgment, Rykon did not doubt River's word. "All right then," he said. "Are we ready to move out?"

After glancing back at the army behind him, River gave a nod.

"We haven't enough ships for everyone to cross at once, I'm afraid," Rykon explained. "We have decided to convene on a stretch of beach where my scouts assure me there are no signs of Ulda's minions."

Aldryg stepped forward and bowed before the king. "Your Majesty, the ships will not be necessary. Lord River?"

"That's correct," River said. "I will summon the elementals in the ocean. With their help, we will march the army across the water's surface."

Rykon stared a moment in stunned silence. "Very well," he finally replied.

River stepped lightly over the sand leading to the shore. White foam splashed against his feet as he stepped into the water, and he felt himself instantly rejuvenated. Voices called out to him from every direction, the song of the elementals filling his soul. Crying out for their aid, he summoned them to his side.

The water's surface glistened before the eyes of the onlookers. A bridge rose from the water, its edges visible by a series of tiny waterfalls, which allowed the excess seawater to drain, allowing for a dry crossing. River emerged from the water momentarily, sending up a fountain of sea spray before diving back into the depths.

"I think that's our signal to follow," Kaiya said.

The combined armies moved forward, placing their feet on the bridge. Though their initial steps were unsteady, they soon realized that the ground was quite solid, and they could easily traverse what should have been an impassable ocean.

River stayed below, replenishing his magic and surfacing only rarely. Soon they would arrive in Ral'nassa, and he would need every ounce of strength he could muster.

Chapter 21

Varl's warning shook Ulda to his core. Locking himself away in his lab, he neither slept nor ate for days. His mind focused only on his research, and he had finally come to a breakthrough. This would mean the difference between success and failure. With the process complete, he would have the most resilient army ever to exist.

Prin made his way slowly up the stairs to his master's lab, hoping the summons had been to inform him of good news. Over the past few days, Ulda had shunned his servant's presence, and Prin was nervous to lay eyes on his master. Knowing full well that no other servant had brought him anything to eat, he feared the sorcerer's condition. Madness had taken hold of him, and Prin did not wish to become part of his experiments.

Knocking twice, he pushed the door open slightly and peered inside.

"Come in, come in!" Ulda's voice called from somewhere inside.

The stench of death hit Prin's nostrils immediately, and he placed his hand over his nose to block it out. Fighting the urge to wretch, Prin moved forward, searching the room with his eyes. Several dead bodies were piled in an alcove, puddles of liquid oozing beneath them. Prin squeezed his eyes shut to block out the vision. He had seen death before, of course, but not like this. Some of the bodies had their flesh ripped away, their lifeless faces frozen in agony. Many of them he recognized as former servants to his master.

"Over here," Ulda called from a dark corner.

Prin's body tensed, his feet glued to the floor. His heart pounded in his ears as he made the decision to move forward. Angering Ulda at this point would not be wise. Whatever the sorcerer had planned for him, he would never be able to escape it. His only choice was to obey.

"Coming, Master," Prin replied, moving through the darkened room.

Kneeling in the corner, her knees hugged to her chest, was a woman. Prin recognized her as a member of the cleaning staff. Her eyes were wide, pleading with him to help her. He could not. Looking away, he finally found his master, who was standing over the woman.

"I have done it!" Ulda shouted in elation. "It is a marvelous thing to behold!"

Prin slowly lowered his hand from his nose and bowed slightly before his master. Taking in the sorcerer's appearance, he could scarcely believe how quickly the man had deteriorated. Always the picture of health and cleanliness, Ulda stood before him now in a state of utter chaos. His features were sunken, with dark lines beneath his eyes. The black robe he wore was wrinkled and stained with various tinctures, and his shoes were nonexistent. Since the sorcerer had not left the laboratory for any reason since becoming obsessed with his research, Prin suspected the stench in the room was due not only to the dead bodies.

"I am happy for you, Master," Prin managed to say. He glanced again at the woman, who had not taken her eyes off him for an instant.

Ulda snapped his fingers, causing Prin to jump. He hoped his master had not noticed this reaction.

"Before I forget," Ulda said as he rushed across the room. Digging in one of his coffers, he threw various items aside. Moving to the next, he repeated the procedure, but found the item he was searching for. "Here," he said, returning to face his servant. In his hand were twelve small white crystals. Dumping them into Prin's open hands, he said, "You must distribute these to my generals. I will use these crystals to issue my orders."

Prin asked, "I thought you intended to be present on the battlefield, Master." It was not his place to question Ulda's actions, but Ulda had said more than once he would face his enemies in the flesh. It seemed his plans had changed.

"I won't be able to," Ulda said, turning around. Looking over at the glowing orb on his table, he said, "I shall have to depend on the orb to see each regiment and how they are faring."

"Understood, Master," Prin responded.

"No, you don't," Ulda snapped. "I haven't shown you yet!" His face grew agitated, and he grunted loudly as he moved to stand in front of the kneeling woman.

"Forgive me, Master," Prin said, hoping to cool the situation. He could easily become next in Ulda's search for lab rats.

Ulda ignored his apology. "This is why I can't be present," he explained. "I have to be here, away from the noise. I must concentrate. The procedure is difficult to perform from a distance." A devious smile spread across the sorcerer's face.

Prin stood solid as ice, his hands clasped behind his back. As he watched, Ulda shot a blast of energy at the woman, causing her neck to bend at an awkward angle. A look of surprise came over her face as she crumpled lifelessly to the floor. Prin resisted the urge to look away.

"But wait!" Ulda shouted, lifting up a finger. A pale yellow glow surrounded the woman's body as she floated a few inches off the ground. As the light faded, she stood on her own feet and looked up at him.

"By all the gods," Prin whispered, his eyes not leaving the sight before him. Rumors of dark magic had been handed down from the ages, but he had never heard of anyone reanimating the dead.

Ulda's face beamed with pride as he turned to face his servant. "I've done it!" he shouted. "She lives once more!"

Prin could not help his fascination. How Ulda had managed such a feat was far beyond his ability to understand, but seeing it right before his eyes was a thing of wonder. Without realizing what he was doing, he reached out his hand to touch the arm of the woman. She felt cold, her skin pale and soft. Looking into her eyes he saw malice but no sign of life. Taking a step back, he withdrew his hand.

"With this technique perfected, my army cannot die," Ulda said, still beaming.

"How many times can you raise the same person?" Prin asked, his voice audibly amazed.

"Infinitely," Ulda said. Shooting another beam of energy at the woman, he slew her a second time. Her head smacked against the floor with an audible crack, blood seeping from the wound. Again the pale yellow light surrounded her, and she rose for a second time. She looked around the room, her dead eyes focusing on Prin.

It was then he noticed that the woman was not breathing. Her chest neither rose nor fell, and her staring eyes did not blink. Prin suspected she was only alive so long as Ulda willed it, but he could not be certain. He glanced over at the other bodies lying in the alcove.

Noticing his servant's gaze, Ulda said, "Those were failed experiments."

"Can you bring them back too?" Prin wondered.

"No," he replied. "I've already extracted their essences for other work."

Turning his focus back to the woman, Prin asked, "Do you have to focus on her permanently in order for her to live?"

Ulda shook his head. "That's the beauty of it. Once she is raised, she acts upon my will until I command her to stop."

"So each person you raise requires your full attention?"

"Not at all," the sorcerer replied. "Before slaying her, I placed an enchantment on her. She is programmed to rise after being killed, and she will slay all Westerling Elves and Na'zorans by any means necessary." He chuckled slightly, adding, "That leaves me free to focus on other matters."

"So your soldiers will resuscitate on their own?" Prin asked.

"Most of them," Ulda replied with a shrug. "The spell is proving more difficult on those who have been hybridized. The standard elven and human soldiers will rise on their own. The creatures I shall raise en masse through the use of my orb."

"Amazing," Prin commented.

"I can't do it from too great a distance," Ulda admitted. "But should a massive tidal wave happen to wipe out my army, I'll be able to raise every one of them."

Prin felt a cold chill run down his spine. The thought of hundreds, perhaps thousands, of undead creatures running around left him unsettled. What would become of them after the battle was won? Would he have to work side by side with them? He shuddered at the thought. These creatures served Ulda in life, and now they would serve him in death. "Master, do you draw out their souls when they are first slain?"

"No," Ulda replied. "I must be present at the moment of death to extract a soul. That would be far too great a strain during battle. I can't possibly be everywhere at once." With a glance at his servant, he added, "Rest assured they will remain bound to my will by this new technique."

"Could another sorcerer bind their souls?" Prin wondered. After all, the elves were known to have magic, and he was aware of at least three master sorcerers coming Ulda's way. They would be killing plenty of Ulda's creations, and they could probably bind essences as easily as his master did. If so, there could be a serious flaw in Ulda's line of thinking.

"The technique of soul extraction is not widely known," Ulda replied. "It is an art form—one that I've perfected. Our enemies have no knowledge of the procedure." Briefly he remembered that Telorithan might be among them. He did have the knowledge, and it brought a twinge of fear to Ulda's mind. Suddenly, River and Kaiya were not the greatest threats to Ulda's plans. "You bring up some interesting ideas, Prin," the sorcerer said. So far his servant had proved useful in a variety of matters. Perhaps he was skilled in battle strategy as well. "Your mind works on levels I hadn't anticipated," the sorcerer admitted

Prin felt uneasy, wondering if he had offended his master. Ulda could snap in a moment, putting an end to his life. "I only wish to be of assistance, Master," Prin said, bowing his head.

"Indeed," Ulda replied. Moving away from his servant, he approached the orb on his table. Willing it to show him River's army, he gazed inside to view the men and women who were approaching. Scanning through their faces, he focused his attention only to the most powerful among them.

River and Kaiya appeared before him, as expected, and the earth mage was there as well. He still did not sense much in the way of magic from him, but he knew how true masters of earth drew their power as needed. Believing he was easily capable of handling these three, he moved on, his eyes finally falling upon Telorithan.

Ulda's body tensed, and he held his breath for a moment before letting it out with a low growl. This man was a threat. He knew Ulda's process for binding a soul, or at least he knew it centuries ago. Focusing his thoughts more intently to Telorithan, he sensed unbalance within the master of fire. Something was wrong with him, as it had been with River. Telorithan's condition was different, however. Ulda did not truly understand it, but he sensed a duality in the elf, which he had never sensed in him before. The sorcerer appeared to have weakened over the years, and this was of great relief to Ulda. Telorithan would not pose the threat he had feared. His success was ensured.

Prin backed away, taking up a position outside his master's door. When Ulda was gazing into the orb, it could take hours. Prin knew his presence would be ignored, whether he stayed or left. Standing in the hallway, he crossed his arms and awaited any orders that might come. At some point, Ulda would have to call for food, and Prin did not want to keep him waiting.

Ignoring the mounting needs of his body, Ulda continued to gaze into the orb. The elves and Na'zorans had combined their strength, and Ulda was surprised by how many soldiers they were bringing. To his count, there were thousands. He hadn't expected that. Apparently the population of Na'zora had grown in the past thirty years. That could be of benefit to Ulda, as he considered them a good source of basic labor.

The army moved with surprising speed, and Ulda realized they must be using magic to aid them in their journey. He laughed to himself, "In a hurry to come and see me, aren't you?" It was of no consequence. Whether they arrived sooner or later, he was ready. His plans were perfected, his army invincible. They would not stand against him for long.

The elemental masters only posed a threat to him should they be able to combine their powers in his presence. With Telorithan weakened, Ulda wasn't certain he still counted as a master of fire. That would have to be determined in person. Though Ulda had no intention of getting near those four. He would stay at a distance, observing them and thwarting their efforts.

It was in his best interest to see that the masters were kept apart. His self-resurrecting army would do just that. Once these masters were aware that their own army was in grave danger, they would have to rush to their aid. That wouldn't leave them much time to break Ulda's defenses and enter his tower.

Continuing to observe the army in his orb, he watched as River dove into the ocean and crafted a bridge for the others to follow. Ulda watched with interest as the soldiers stepped onto the ocean's surface and found it solid. Chuckling to himself, he said, "Nice trick, but it won't save you."

Ulda sat back, certain that his victory was at hand. The stress and anxiety he had felt over the past few days was fading. All he had to do now was wait.

Chapter 22

Ulda's tower stood imposing in the distance as the

army approached Ral'nassa. Gathering their forces on the beach, the units made ready for the attack. River, Kaiya, Mel, and Telorithan stood together, charting the path they would take to the tower.

Isandra strode to her father's side, knowing his destination. "I will escort you to the tower," she said, her sword already drawn.

River knew better than to deny her the privilege. Even if he protested, she would insist on cutting a path for her father to traverse safely. Swallowing his argument, he nodded his acceptance of her offer.

King Rykon joined them, his eyes burning with the fire of revenge. "We will provide cover for you," he said. "Whatever happens, Ulda must be stopped."

The army's arrival had not gone unnoticed. Fell creatures gathered in droves, awaiting the prey that had walked so willingly into their land. Howls rang out as the creatures taunted the invaders. A single, piercing shriek cut through the humans and elves, who focused their attention to the sky, where riders perched atop massive wyverns circled.

"Looks like Ulda's been busy these past thirty years," Mel commented. He had not encountered such creatures in the last battle against Ulda.

Telorithan let out a low unnerving laugh. Summoning the fire within, his eyes flashed red as he released a wide burst of fire in the monsters' direction. The creatures scattered, some of them crying out in pain as the fireball exploded in their midst.

"That's the best he can create?" Telorithan asked, laughing once more.

"His creatures might not be a threat to you," River began, "but he certainly is."

Lifting his hand to throw a second fireball, Telorithan's eyes flashed red. River reached up, grabbing the sorcerer's arm, a cloud of steam rising between them. "We're here to save these people if we can, not kill as many as possible."

"You can't be serious," Telorithan replied.

River stared into his eyes, his expression severe.

Shaking his head, Telorithan said, "I know what it would require to release all these bound souls." He paused a moment to look at the creatures. "It would take an immense sacrifice."

"I'm aware of that," River replied. "We have to try. The people trapped inside those monsters are innocent."

Without any argument, Telorithan shrugged. If River, Mel, and Kaiya planned to sacrifice themselves to save these people, so be it.

Reaching into his bag, River produced the red gem and handed it to the fire sorcerer. Telorithan's eyes blazed red as he gazed upon it, its warmth searing his hand. His mind swam with all the possibilities, and the unlimited powers this stone could bestow upon him. With this gem, he could realize his ultimate dream—to hold the power of a god.

Seeing the lust in Telorithan's eyes, River said, "Lorith, I can see that you are weary." Reaching out, he placed a hand on the sorcerer's shoulder. "We are both weary," he said. "Our time in this world is ending." With his mind, he projected his thoughts to Telorithan's mind, reminding him of the gravity of the situation. If Ulda succeeded, he would control the world, and he would take Telorithan's power for his own. The fire sorcerer knew he could not stand alone against the power of the fifth element. Even the gemstone would not protect him.

Slowly, Telorithan's red eyes returned to blue. "Lorith is weary," he whispered. "Ulda must be stopped."

To Mel, it appeared that River had cast a spell over the sorcerer, but he knew River to be incapable of manipulation. He attempted to glimpse inside Telorithan's mind, but the duality he saw there only left him confused. There was great strength inside him, but there was also a feeling of exhaustion—of an ancient soul prepared to rest.

"We must be on our way," River said. Turning to Rykon, he added, "Your army must fight on, no matter what monsters appear before you. The four of us must get to Ulda as quickly as possible. We won't be able to assist you."

"And we mustn't be interrupted once we reach the tower," Kaiya added.

"I understand," Rykon replied. "Do as you must. My army will stop these creatures from reaching you."

To his companions, River said, "We must make our way to the tower, regardless of what occurs behind us.

Ignore everything you see. Focus only on reaching the tower."

"That won't be a problem," Kaiya said. Her eyes sparkling silver, she blasted a path between the waiting creatures, knocking them to the ground.

Taking advantage of his enemies as they scrambled to their feet, Rykon sounded the charge. The Na'zorans raced forward, trampling and slashing at the monsters before them. The elves followed close behind, engaging the enemy on foot.

Mel watched in amazement as the creatures fell, surrounded by a yellow glow. When the monsters rose from death, he could scarcely believe his eyes. "Ulda's raising the dead!" he shouted.

"There's nothing we can do about it," River said, his own eyes taking in the spectacle. Fear ran through his body, but it would not stop him. His destination was clear, and his mission was not yet complete. "Come on!" he shouted.

The four wizards ran forward, Isandra charging a few steps ahead of them. Wolfmen lay hidden in tall patches of spiky grass, ready to pounce as their prey moved closer. Leaping onto the path, they snarled and slashed with their claws. Kaiya maneuvered around Isandra, hurling energy blasts at the beasts.

Isandra noticed a striped creature running directly for her, and she raised her sword to the ready. It leapt at her, fangs bared, a low growl in its throat. Swinging with precision, she landed her sword directly where its neck should have been, but the cat was too agile. It twisted its lithe body, narrowly avoiding the sword and landing safely a few inches from the warrior.

Before she could swing again, Mel reached into the earth, calling to the animal portion of the hybridized beast. He could sense the tormented will of the bound elf but pushed it aside. Ulda's hold on the elf was far too strong. The beast still had a primal instinct. Mel focused his mind to the animal, warning it that a danger had come that was too great to stand against. The tiger ran away from the battle, fleeing for its life.

River turned to Mel and nodded, acknowledging the earth master's mercy.

Nearly halfway to the tower, the wyvern circled again, preparing to swoop on the invaders. Kaiya reacted quickly, her eyes flashing silver as she forced the wyvern to alter its course with a burst of air. The beast's rider was ready, casting a quick spell to steady himself and the wyvern. Turning high in the air, he prepared for another attack.

Blasting another burst of air, Kaiya said, "We have to hurry. This isn't going to hold him off for long."

The group broke into a run, heading straight for the base of the tower. Thick vines of ivy covered the stonework, but Mel was quick to spot a single door. Gently moving the vines away, he said, "I hope this opens."

A shriek of anger sounded from above as the wyvern dipped low in the sky. River cast a blue shield to protect his companions from the impending attack. Kaiya turned to the door, summoning an energy blast in her hands and hurling it toward the stone. The door glowed momentarily before a deep purple mist shrouded the frame. As the color grew deeper, it swirled and reached away from the tower, focusing its energy on the intruders.

"Move!" Kaiya shouted as she rolled to the side.

River's shield dropped as he and the others threw themselves out of harm's way. A thunderous crash ripped through the air, shaking the earth beneath their feet. Kaiya's energy spell bounced back from the door, spinning wildly and hurling sparks in every direction.

Mel reacted quickly, digging deep into the earth with his mind. Lifting the sand to smother the spell, he slowed it down, but could not stop it.

River returned to his feet and focused his mind to the sand-covered ball of energy that was making its way toward Kaiya. His eyes flashed blue as he unleashed his magic, encompassing the rogue spell with the full strength of his element. It sputtered only a few seconds longer before dissolving into a heap of wet sand.

Telorithan was the only one watching as the wyvern once again focused on the group. It reared its reptilian head, baring its fangs as it dove at them. Holding his hand outward, a beam of orange light connected with the beast, and it screeched in pain. The sorcerer atop its back was no mere apprentice. He too was a master of fire and knew how to counter Telorithan's spell. Projecting his own beam of red magic, he destabilized the spell that held his mount, sending him reeling high into the air.

Telorithan dropped briefly to one knee, a look of surprise on his face. Glancing at River, he said, "It looks like I underestimated my opponent." He would never accept that he was, indeed, beginning to weaken. Instead, he chose to believe that his years of solitude had diminished his skills in wizard's duels. It had been too long since he encountered any other being of magical design. Assuming them all to be below him in their skills, he hadn't bothered to assess the strength of Ulda or his followers.

As she watched the wyvern circling back, Kaiya said, "Someone is going to have to lead him off. We need time to get this door open!" Growing impatient with the constant interruptions, she was ready to rip the beast's head off, either with magic or with her bare hands.

"I will," Isandra declared, her sword still held at the ready.

River felt an ache in his heart but withheld the fatherly lecture. Though it pained him to put his child in such grave danger, he could not risk harm coming to Mel, Kaiya, or Telorithan. Without them, there was no hope of stopping Ulda. He swallowed hard, feeling a tightness in his throat. With a deep breath, he reminded himself that his daughter was among the finest warriors present this day. He decided it was best to let her try. If anyone here could defeat the wyvern and its master, it was Isandra.

River embraced his daughter, holding her close to his chest. His robe offered little protection from the hardness of her plate armor, but he ignored his discomfort and clutched her tightly. With a soft kiss on her cheek, he released her, spreading blue enchantment over her armor. "It will protect you," he said, his voice cracking slightly.

Mel and Kaiya focused energy to Isandra's sword, and it glowed with a multitude of colors as she turned it over in her hand. Nodding her thanks, she turned back to her father. "I wish you luck," she said. "We will meet again." Her eyes portrayed her confidence that she would, indeed, survive this battle.

"You are the strength of our family now," River said solemnly. "You will always have my love." Placing his hand against her face, he added, "Fight well, my daughter."

Isandra leaned in and kissed her father's cheek with surprising softness. She understood his words completely. Fighting back the tears that insisted on welling in her eyes, she lifted her sword high in the air, pointing its tip at the circling wyvern. With a fierce cry, she charged toward the battle, her armor and sword leaving a trail of colored magic behind her. With these enchantments, the mounted sorcerer saw her as the most immediate threat to his master and changed his course to pursue.

River forced himself to turn his face away from Isandra as she fought. Mel and Kaiya set to work, attempting to blast open the door that would lead them to Ulda.

Noticing the look of distress on River's face, Telorithan moved to his side "Soon we will both be free," he said.

"We must do what is necessary," River said in a whisper. His heart was in more turmoil with his daughter present. Though she was a fierce warrior, he worried for her safety, especially now. This enemy was greater than any she had faced. He must reach Ulda as quickly as possible, and end this once and for all.

Kaiya stepped away from the door, having done all she could do. Now it was Mel's turn. She took the opportunity to approach Telorithan. "Just in case I don't make it out of there," she began, "I have to know what really convinced you to help us."

A crooked smile appeared on the sorcerer's lips. "Simple," he said. "Ulda is an arrogant ass. He believes himself the greatest wizard who has ever lived. He's wrong. I am the greatest wizard who ever lived."

Kaiya couldn't suppress a laugh. "Confident to the last," she said, shaking her head.

"While we're on the subject," Telorithan added, "I still hate you."

Kaiya shrugged, her smile not leaving her face. "I bested you, and you can't stand it," she said smugly.

"You caught me unaware," he shot back. "I had already spent the vast majority of my magical stores, and you took advantage of that."

"I could face you at full strength," she said, staring him in the eye.

"I haven't the energy to fight you if I'm going to face Ulda," Telorithan replied. "I have to choose who deserves my wrath more. Ulda needs to be taken down a notch." Narrowing his eyes, he added, "Besides, he is a more worthy opponent than you."

Kaiya ignored the comment but peered into his mind. Finding it less protected than before, she felt as if he wanted her to see what he was thinking. A deep sense of respect was emanating from the sorcerer, and it caught her by surprise. She felt certain she was reading him correctly. Though the bitterness was still there, deep down, he respected Kaiya, and not only for the fact that she had beaten him. It was unfathomable that a woman could be more powerful than him, and the fact that the woman was a dwarf had added further insult. He had had time to contemplate their encounter, and he had come to marvel at her abilities.

She was a thing unexpected, and he had thought about her many times over the years.

Backing out of his mind, Kaiya remained silent about what she had seen. Telorithan was not to be crossed, and she would not mock him. Seeing inside his thoughts had reminded her that he was, after all, still a person. He was far less a villain than he had been in his youth.

"Got it!" Mel announced, snapping Kaiya back to reality.

The four of them watched as the stone door swung open, revealing the spiral staircase within. Exchanging glances, they readied themselves for the challenge ahead.

River stepped inside first, peering inside the dimly lit corridor. At first glance, there was no sign of any resistance. That was sure to change once Ulda became aware they had entered. River stood to one side of the doorway, gesturing for his friends to follow.

"This is probably a bad time to ask this," Mel said, looking up to the top of the spire, "but without my feet in direct contact with the earth, how am I supposed to cast earth magic spells?"

Kaiya sighed. "Yes, this is a bad time to ask," she said. "You really should learn to think a few steps ahead. Even animals can do that." She grinned at Mel, but he did not appear to appreciate her joke.

"You will have to dig deeper than usual," River replied. "I have every confidence in you."

Mel wasn't so sure. He had never performed magic from high in the air. Ulda's tower looked to be at least fifteen stories high.

Abandoning her attempts at humor, Kaiya placed a comforting hand on Mel's arm. "I will manipulate the air, easing the resistance you'll encounter while you try to tap into the earth," she explained. "Once you've done so, River will have an easier time tapping into the water beneath the ground, and Telorithan can reach deeper into the fire."

"We must work together if we are to succeed," River added. "Each of us is essential."

Mel nodded, acknowledging that he understood. Trying to ease his mounting anxiety, he slapped Kaiya gently on the shoulder. "Looks like you're the most important person here," he said.

Waving her hand dismissively, she said, "I'm just getting things started."

Stepping inside the doorway, Mel wondered how they were going to keep Ulda under control long enough for everyone to cast the spells they needed to cast. Choosing not to ask for fear of the answer, he continued on in silence.

Before stepping inside, Kaiya turned her head back toward the battle. Her eyes landed on one of Ulda's warriors who was lying on the ground surrounded by a yellow light. As she watched, he rose to his feet, readying his weapon to fight again. Her eyes widened as she turned back to her companions, still in disbelief that Ulda had mastered such dark magic.

River noticed her discomfort and motioned her to come inside. "There is only one way to help them," he said. "We must complete our mission."

Taking a deep breath, Kaiya stepped inside the corridor. Telorithan followed close behind her, the door slamming shut as he entered. A pale glow of silver light shone around its edges, sealing the door in place.

Chapter 23

Isandra led the wyvern away from her father's location, the magic on her armor leaving a trail of colorful sparks for the creature to follow. Halfway between the tower and the thick of battle, she halted, readying her sword. The decision to fight here was based purely on logic. She was close enough to her allies that her battle would not go unnoticed. Should she fall, another would likely pick up where she left off, stopping the creature from heading straight back to River and his companions. There was little else she could do for him.

As the wyvern approached, Isandra forced thoughts of her father from her mind. His words had sounded so final, and she knew he did not expect to survive his encounter with Ulda. All she could do was hope he was wrong—that he would live, and the two of them would spend many more days together.

Positioning her feet apart and bending slightly at the knees, Isandra steeled herself for the wyvern's attack. The sorcerer atop the beast crouched low, bracing himself for an impact as well. Isandra knew what was coming. The beast lunged its weight forward, closing on her position. On instinct, she twisted her body, narrowly avoiding a collision.

She spun to watch as the wyvern made a tight circle, its sights once again set on her. Readying herself, she lifted her sword. This time, the creature flew inches from her body, the sorcerer sending out a blast of white sparks. Isandra was hit, the magic burning dark spots on her armor and diminishing the blue glow her father had placed over her. The sorcerer was trying to remove her magical defenses.

Despite its massive size, the creature was surprisingly agile. It glided on the wind, tilting its tail slightly to maneuver back into position. Isandra was ready. Holding her sword firmly, she poised to strike as soon as the wyvern was within reach. Before her eyes, the beast split in two, one attacking from her left, the other to her right. With no time to decide which was the bigger threat, Isandra swung her sword at the beast on the left. Her sword penetrated the image, and it disappeared before her. *An illusion*, she realized too late. The real wyvern crashed into her, bowling her over.

With her face pressed into the dirt, Isandra attempted to right herself. Swooping down, the wyvern grabbed her in its talons. She grabbed the hilt of her sword only an instant before she was hoisted into the air. The beast thrashed its leg, shaking the elf like a ragdoll. Isandra clung to the scaled leg, her head spinning from the motion.

The sorcerer leaned over the side of his mount, looking into Isandra's eyes. His visage was dark, his expression one of pure hatred. She could feel his malevolence and his sincere desire to crush her. Gripping her tighter in its talons, the wyvern squeezed with all its strength, but it could not penetrate her enchanted armor. It cried out in anger, reeling its head.

Isandra saw her moment to act. With a swift move, she struck at the talons, the runes of her sword flashing in a multitude of colors. In a single swipe, she sliced through one of the long scaly toes, watching as it dropped from the air and landed somewhere out of sight.

Crying out in pain, the creature jerked to one side, momentarily knocking the sorcerer off balance. As he swung her direction, Isandra thrust her sword at him. She heard nothing, but saw the tip of her sword dripping with blood. With regret, she realized the wound would not be deep, nor would it be life threatening. Clutching tightly to the wyvern's leg, she attempted to climb up its scales.

Noticing that the elf warrior was approaching, the sorcerer prepared another spell. A wave of energy washed over her, forcing her to lose her grip from the beast's foot. It took great effort to avoid dropping her sword, but Isandra instinctively tightened her grip as the energy crashed into her. Her other hand slipped from the scales, and for an instant, she was falling freely into the sky. As the beast's tail moved into view, she grabbed on, narrowly avoiding a fall to her death. Peering at the ground below, the soldiers were too small to be seen. All she could make out were small puffs of smoke, likely caused by magical fire.

Climbing along the wyvern's tail, Isandra had a good view of its underbelly. On most creatures, this area would be soft and vulnerable. Unfortunately, she could find no such spot on this creature. Its entire body was armored with thick, golden scales. In vain, she stabbed at the scales, hoping to find a soft place between them where the beast could be injured.

Swiveling his head, the sorcerer took notice of the elf who was still clutching to the wyvern's tail. He had thought her finished, but still she persisted. Raising his hand, he prepared a blast of fire. Unleashing the magic from his hand, he projected it at her and waited for her screams to reach his ears.

As nimble as a lemur, the woman swung gracefully under the tail, shielding herself from the fiery attack. The magic glinted off the wyvern's scales, bouncing to the ground below. In anger, the sorcerer pulled hard on the wyvern's reins, knocking it slightly off-balance. It swooped low, giving Isandra the opportunity she needed. With a gentle leap, she flung herself from the creature's tail, somersaulting onto the ground and bouncing back onto her feet. Readying her sword, she prepared for the beast to circle back.

With a piercing shriek, the monster homed in on her position. Standing her ground, she waited until the moment was right before stepping gracefully to the side. The sorcerer hurled another fireball, but Isandra's sword caught it midair. The runed blade flashed with a blue light as the fire dissipated in a puff of steam. The sorcerer's eyes went wide as he stared at where his fireball had been. Isandra didn't hesitate. She swung her sword again, slashing at the rider, mortally wounding him. He toppled from the beast, landing hard on the ground, a pool of dark blood surrounding him.

The monster cried out at the death of its master, diving on Isandra's position and knocking her off her feet. Grabbing at its injured talon, she righted herself, and positioned her sword to strike. *Somewhere this creature must have a weakness*, she thought. It thrashed its leg, attempting to force the woman to release her grip, but Isandra held fast. She studied the underbelly once more, but still found it impenetrable. Looking up, she realized there was a slight break in the plating where the scales of its legs met the scales of its torso. She had not noticed this before. Hoping she had finally found a soft spot, Isandra thrust her sword upward, penetrating the wyvern between its scales.

The creature's earsplitting cry let her know she had succeeded. Thrusting the sword farther still, she pushed with all her might. Blood sprayed from the wound, the flow increasing as she twisted her blade.

The wyvern rocked and weaved, spreading its massive wings as if to take to the air, but the creature had little strength left. Isandra's attack had found an artery, and the beast had lost too much blood to continue the fight. Slowly, it limped, dragging its injured leg as it attempted to escape its doom. Isandra pulled her sword free, unleashing a torrent of blood. Within seconds, the beast ceased to move, its final breath escaping its lungs in a long, mournful sigh.

Isandra turned toward the tower, hoping her father and his companions were safe. For a moment, she thought of returning to see if he needed further assistance, but she discerned no movement near the tower's base. It was likely he was already inside. Turning back to the battle raging on behind her, she knew where her help was most needed.

King Rykon, whose gold-embellished helmet left no question as to how important he was, stood surrounded by servants of the enemy. Heavily armored soldiers closed in around him as he held his father's sword high. Isandra hurried through the thick of battle, slashing at everything in her path. The king would not fall if she could reach him in time.

Slashing in an arcing motion, Rykon cut through the soldiers closest to him. Spinning around, he crossed swords with one soldier, blocking the attack that was aimed for his back. Struggling against the soldier's strength, Rykon forced his sword upward, slamming the pommel into the man's chin. He staggered backward, giving Rykon the opening he needed to finish him. With a thrust of his blade, he ran the soldier through. The man fell to the ground, but no blood pooled beneath him.

A look of relief came over Rykon's face as he saw Isandra approaching. She cut down three soldiers in her path before coming to the king's side.

"It's good to see you," he said.

Isandra did not respond. Her eyes were locked on the man at Rykon's feet. A yellow glow encircled him, and he slowly made his way back to his feet, using his hands to support him on the way up.

Rykon slashed again, relieving the man of his head. "Every soldier and creature we kill comes back to life," he told her. "It's an impossible fight, but we'll hold them as long as we can."

Isandra could see that the king had spoken true. The decapitated body was searching the ground for its severed head. At her approach, the head growled and gnashed its teeth. Stepping forward, she kicked the head farther away, the body scrambling to follow. "There has to be a way to stop them," she said.

"The mages can blast them to bits, but a sword is all but useless. I'm all ears if you have a suggestion."

Before he could speak more, the soldiers he had previously cut down were coming after him again. Their wounds were still visible, but the blood had ceased to run, and they appeared no worse for wear. Their swords held high, they rejoined the battle, challenging the Na'zoran king.

With a fierce cry, Isandra charged at the soldiers, the king swinging wildly at her side. Together they cut through the line, sending the men to their deaths once more. Their bodies slid lifelessly to the ground, crumpling without a sound.

Rykon stood over them, breathing heavily. "They'll get back up," he said. "I've been working on this same group since we arrived." As he spoke, one of the bodies suddenly sprung to its feet, hurling itself onto the king's back. He staggered forward, surprised by the sudden attack. Isandra grabbed the man by his shoulders, violently slamming him to the ground and stabbing her sword through his neck.

"Like I said," Rykon said, shrugging slightly.

As the yellow light engulfed the bodies of the fallen, Isandra could bear no more. Slicing madly at the men, she hacked off limbs, heads, and exposed the corpses' inner workings. Flesh rained down upon her, a shower of disgusting proportions. Rykon shielded his eyes as the elf warrior continued hacking away. Finally, she stepped back to observe her work.

"This would go easier with an axe," she commented, wiping the blood away from her face.

Rykon stared into the mass Isandra had created. The yellow light came and went, but the soldiers did not rise. They had no legs or arms to do so. Instead, the masses of flesh quivered and pulsated as they tried desperately to obey their master's morbid command.

"Shred them to ribbons," Rykon said. "A time-consuming solution, but effective." He managed a smile at this small victory.

Isandra nodded once. "Let's get to work on the rest of them," she said. Lifting her runed sword high, she charged into the battle that raged all around her, followed closely by the king.

Chapter 24

Stepping cautiously along the dimly lit corridor, the companions encountered no resistance. All was silent within the tower, and a single light shone brightly, illuminating the spiral staircase ahead of them. The soft glow was warm, almost inviting. Their senses on high alert, they moved toward the light.

The narrow corridor made movement difficult when they tried to walk side by side. For comfort, they walked single file with River in the lead and Mel bringing up the rear. His head swiveled constantly, expecting an attack from behind at any moment. His heart pounded in his ears, each breath rapid and shallow.

No sound could be heard save the soft footfalls of the four intruders. River moved with an easy caution, his apprehension seeming to dull as they moved closer to the staircase. It surprised him that he wasn't more nervous. He was about to face the greatest challenge of his life—the man who had murdered the Spirit who gave him life. The task before him would require immense effort, but River's resolve was true. Leaving his family behind had been the most difficult part, and that was over. There was only one more thing he could do to protect them.

Stepping into the light, River's shadow fell across his companions. As his foot touched the first step, a white light flashed before him, sending up a blast of energy. Knocked off balance, River crashed backward, landing hard against the stone floor. Mel and Kaiya shielded their eyes momentarily from the sparks, but Telorithan seemed unaffected. He stooped low over River, extending his hand.

Acting purely on instinct, Kaiya inserted herself between the two elves, her eyes focused on Telorithan. She did not trust him, and this would be an easy time to do River harm if that was the sorcerer's intention. Instead, Telorithan maneuvered his arm around Kaiya, extending his hand once again to help River to his feet. River graciously accepted, giving a soft look to Kaiya, who still appeared suspicious.

Mel cut through the tense moment by pointing out River's injury. "You're bleeding," he said, pointing to his own forehead.

River touched the wound with his fingers and said, "It's only a minor scratch."

"I'll take the lead," Telorithan said, his eyes flashing red. "I believe I'll have an easier time spotting any more traps."

River nodded, allowing the sorcerer to walk in front of him as the group continued climbing the stairs. After only a few steps, Telorithan paused, pointing a finger at an unseen device near the wall.

"There's another one," he said.

Kaiya stretched her neck to see around the others, her keen eyes spotting what the sorcerer had seen. Carved in yellow magic was a single rune, one that she did not recognize. It was barely noticeable, tucked between two slabs of stone.

Summoning the fire within, Telorithan's eyes flashed red. "Take cover," he commanded them. His companions crouched near the wall, shielding themselves with their arms. Unleashing red magic, Telorithan blasted the rune, sending yellow sparks and bits of stone tearing through the air. When the dust settled, he grinned at the others. It had been far too long since he destroyed anything with fire. Though this had been on a small scale, he still enjoyed the sound the fire made as it ripped through the trap, reducing it to ashes.

The invaders continued up the stairs, watching every inch of stone for another trap. To their surprise, they found none.

In a whisper, Kaiya asked, "Why would Ulda place only two traps, neither of which posed any real threat?"

Mel shrugged. "Maybe he wasn't expecting us."

"He is," River said, "but that isn't why he's not trying to stop us." He looked upward along the spiral staircase. "He wants us to come."

Boldly, Kaiya said, "Then that will be his undoing."

River looked back at her, the worry on his face softening. Kaiya had been strong since the first time they met, many centuries ago. He admired her courage, her determination to defend what was just no matter what she had to face. "I believe it will," he agreed.

Mel wasn't so sure, but he kept his doubts to himself. All of the others had centuries of magical study on him. He knew he was the weakest link here, and if their mission failed, it would likely be due to his own shortcomings. His only option was to draw strength from those around him, knowing that they probably needed little help from him.

River turned to Mel and said, "I am not reading your thoughts, but I see the doubt in your heart. You are a child of earth magic, born of the forest. The power within you will not be denied."

Mel seemed puzzled. "I'm not denying that I have some powers," he said. "I just don't think it's anywhere near your level."

River smiled at his friend. "Many things hold us back in this life," he said. "We must learn to overcome those things which prevent us from living as we were meant to. Unleash the power, Mel. Let it soar freely, and allow yourself to fly alongside it."

Hearing those words, Mel felt a warmth burning inside his chest. Ever since learning he was a shaman, he had been frightened. There was much he didn't understand, and he was afraid of trying too hard and not succeeding. He had convinced himself that magic didn't come naturally to him, that he was just some freak of nature. If River was correct, Mel was born to create magic. All he had to do was stop fighting it and allow the magic to flow.

Kaiya suppressed a laugh, squeezing her eyes tightly shut. "I think he's getting it now," she whispered. "I went through similar doubts of my own, Mel. But the feeling I get when the magic channels through me is beyond anything I can describe."

Telorithan crossed his arms impatiently. "If we're done with the little pep talk, might we continue?"

"This one has never doubted himself," Kaiya said, gesturing her thumb at the sorcerer.

Snapping his head around to face her, he replied, "Of course I have. Only a fool believes himself infallible." Continuing up the stairs, he added, "Fools like this Ulda."

As the top of the stairs came into view, a single individual stood near a wooden door, his hands held tightly together in front of him. Prin was the only remaining servant in Ulda's tower, having chosen to remain to the last.

Only moments ago Prin heard what sounded like voices, and he knew Ulda's enemies were closing in. Pounding on the door, he implored his master to flee, but Ulda had refused. His only response had been, "You are dismissed," a comment that wounded the servant.

Weeks ago, Prin believed his master was wholly capable of winning this fight. But his recent descent into madness as he pored over his studies to create his undying army had changed him. No longer did he appear strong and imposing. His mannerisms still had the same cocky air, but his weary appearance betrayed the truth.

Prin could not help feeling some fondness for the man. After all, it was only thanks to Ulda that Prin had collected his wealth. Regardless of Ulda's victory, Prin had the means to live a long, comfortable life. At this final moment, he was surprised to find himself still hoping for his master to succeed. Prin could be the second most powerful man in all Nōl'Deron.

Standing his ground as the four sorcerers approached, Prin took in a deep breath and held it. "My master is engaged," he said, his voice refusing to crack. "You are not permitted an audience with him."

Kaiya lunged forward, her patience gone. Grabbing Prin by his waist, she flipped him over her shoulder, slamming him wide-eyed to the ground. "I *will* be visiting your master today. My friends and I come bearing justice. No longer will he terrorize the people of this land. This is your chance to get out of here in one piece. He controls you now, but once you are relieved of him, you'll be glad you took my offer."

Prin stared up at her, her gray eyes flashing with flecks of silver. Swallowing hard, he said, "I cannot leave my master."

"Stay then," she replied. "If you interfere, I will kill you." Her voice revealed no deception. No one would stand in her way. She was ready for this duty to be completed, and for the world to be free once more.

Prin rose slowly to his knees, his eyes taking in each of the intruders. Though Kaiya had threatened him, he could not see such a small woman doing him great harm. River's eyes held only kindness and pity, and Prin knew the elf would not touch him. As he looked at Mel, he sensed a familiar feeling—anxiety. But as his eyes met Telorithan's fiery gaze, a tingle ran down Prin's spine. Here was true malice, buried deep within the body of an elf. Ulda had been right to fear this man.

Climbing to his feet, Prin glanced only once at the door that would lead him to his master. Then, in an instant, he bolted, panic spreading throughout his body. Running down the stairs, he moved as quickly as possible. At the bottom of the staircase, the stone door swung open, allowing the servant his freedom. He did not look back.

Turning his attention to the door, River laid a hand on the latch. With a nod to his companions, he turned the handle. Opening with no resistance, as River knew it would, the elf stepped inside the room. Telorithan stepped boldly behind him, Mel and Kaiya exchanging glances before following.

"Welcome," Ulda's voice called from within. He stood with his shoulders stooped, peering into the orb upon his desk.

"End this," River said in a calm tone. "There is a peaceful resolution, if only you will allow it."

Ulda turned to view his visitors, a crooked smile upon his lips. "I'm surprised you've come to me directly," he said. "Your army is on the verge of defeat, but it seems you care not for their lives. Your own daughter is near death."

"He's lying," Kaiya shot back.

Unshaken, River said, "It doesn't have to end this way, Ulda."

Stepping forward, Ulda said, "You think I feel threatened by your presence? You are nothing to me!" With a wave of his hand, he blasted a stream of magic at his opponents, its colors shimmering in a multitude of hues.

River conjured a shield to protect his companions, but it could not withstand Ulda's attack. The magic absorbed into the shield momentarily before it burst, sending a shower of blue sparks raining down. As the others attempted to block Ulda's spell, Kaiya crafted a whirlwind, its silver energy inhaling the magic being thrown at it.

Ulda ceased his attack and laughed. "That was a mere trifle," he said. Casting a wide spell, he knocked the entire party off their feet, and sent himself careening backward.

Scampering to his feet, River cried to the others, "Your gems! Use them!" Drawing the blue gem, River gripped it by its base with his fingers. Focusing his energy through its facets, he concentrated only on holding Ulda in place. Telorithan joined in, mirroring River's actions with his red stone. Ulda's shocked expression told the others that the spell was working.

Retrieving her crystal, Kaiya knelt and closed her eyes. Focusing on the air around her, she pulled its energy through the stone. As it unleashed a blast of silver at Ulda, Kaiya was startled, momentarily losing her concentration. Ulda seized the opportunity to break free.

Moving with agility uncommon to a man of his age, Ulda managed to dodge Kaiya's second attempt at containing him. Grabbing his orb from the desk, he held it in his outstretched arms toward Telorithan. The red gem shook violently, catching the sorcerer off guard. In a shower of red sparks, it flew from his hand, sliding across the floor near Ulda.

Ulda lashed out at the stunned sorcerer, blasting him with a yellow beam. The air from Telorithan's lungs was stolen away, an intense weight pressing against his chest. Beneath the crushing blow, the sorcerer buckled to his knees. As he struggled for breath, Kaiya regained her focus, sending a blast of silver through Ulda's midsection. Staggering sideways, he lost his grip on the orb, freeing Telorithan from his grasp.

River and Kaiya held fast to Ulda as Telorithan righted himself and retrieved his gem. Crossing close to Ulda, he stared into the sorcerer's eyes. "I see your fear," Telorithan said.

"And…I see yours," Ulda managed to say through a clenched jaw.

Manipulating the air, Kaiya continued to focus her energy to the space around her. Cutting through the energies that separated Mel from the earth, she allowed him to begin his portion of the spell.

Mel knelt facing Kaiya, as his instinct told him to do. His back to Ulda, he focused his mind away from the sorcerer and into the earth. Finding an easy path to the ground, he silently gave thanks to Kaiya's mastery of air magic. Clutching the gem tightly, he attempted to tap into the earth's magic. His fear of failure ever present, he felt himself unable to pull energy through the stone. *I can't do this*, he realized. *I'm not strong enough*. The harder he tried, the more separated from the earth he became. His breath came swifter as panic set in. *They will fail because of you,* a voice said in his mind. Certain it was Ulda speaking, Mel steeled himself and tried again. Pulling at the earth's energy, he felt himself waning. His magic stores were diminishing, and he was not near enough to the ground to replenish them.

Another voice entered Mel's head—the calm and ever-comforting voice of River. *Allow the magic to flow,* his voice said. Hoping for the best, Mel took in a deep breath and let it out slowly. Focusing his mind away from the gravity of the situation and forgetting that all of Nōl'Deron was in his hands, Mel freed himself from the burden of the world. Allowing his mind to wander, he thought only of his forest home. Visions of trees and tall grass came into his mind, bringing him a sense of peace. His heart swelled with love for the forest, and he drew its energy inside him. The emerald in his hands lit up, a beam of green light stretching out to encompass Ulda.

River didn't waste a moment tapping into the water hiding deep within the earth. Pulling it through his body, he felt himself rejuvenated by its presence. The great supply of magic he had used to hold Ulda in place was replenished, allowing him to strike out at the sorcerer. A blue beam of light shot through Ulda, his expression twisting to one of pain.

With three elements against him, the sorcerer's weakened frame was becoming unstable. He knew he must act now, or he would not survive. Summoning the fifth element, he tapped into the energy of the void. The room darkened, and violet sparks rained down from the ceiling. Kaiya, Mel, and River braced themselves, refusing to lose concentration. Ulda pulled stronger at the void, desperately trying to stop the attackers. Realizing it was futile to attempt all four at once, he focused his energy to Mel, whom he considered the weakest of the group.

River allowed a part of his magic to break away from Ulda long enough to cover Mel's head with a shield of light. It would prevent Ulda from breaking Mel's concentration, but River could not hold the spell for long. It was now up to Telorithan to finish the job.

Gripping the red gem firmly in his fingers, Telorithan focused his energy to the fiery heart of the world. Into the very core he dug, allowing the fire to consume his soul. The elemental inside cried out in rage, its malice and desire to consume life erupting to the surface. Lorith, the elf who had almost ceased to exist, felt himself awakened, and a sincere desire for release consumed his mind.

Telorithan's body lit up with red flame as he leapt toward the bound Ulda. In a blinding flash, both men evaporated, leaving behind a pile of multicolored gems. River dashed to the gems, kneeling among them and pulling them toward his person. Within these gems were the souls of those Ulda had used to create his powers—mighty wizards whose essences the evil sorcerer had collected. Only River could set them free of their torment.

Tapping his blue gem against the pile of bound souls, he spread blue energy over them. Focusing his mind only to releasing all those who had been bound, the pile of gems began to shake. Kaiya and Mel focused their minds to this task as well, their combined efforts sending a shockwave throughout the tower. The structure shook violently, sending bits of stone and sand crumbling from the ceiling.

Pulling energy from the water inside himself, River pictured Lenora's face. A single tear came to his eye as he bid silent farewell to his love. A fleeting glimpse of his children appeared only moments before he disappeared in a flash of blue, taking the bound souls along with him.

Kaiya dropped the gem in her hand and watched in stunned silence as it melted away to nothingness. Mel's gem evaporated as well, his eyes staring at where it had once been.

Looking around the room, he asked, "What's happened to River and Telorithan?" In his heart he knew the answer.

Kaiya stared where River had knelt among the gems. "They sacrificed themselves," she said quietly. "It was the only way." She swallowed the lump rising in her throat.

Suddenly angry, Mel replied, "No! It was Ulda who was supposed to be sacrificed!"

Kaiya shook her head and looked up at her companion. "Ulda had to die, or he never would have stopped enslaving innocent people," she explained. "The elemental inside Lorith was the only creature with the ability to destroy him." Looking at the floor, she added, "River sacrificed himself to free the souls in the gems. They lived in torment long enough." Tears welled in her eyes, and she did not look up.

Mel rose to his feet and moved to the tower window. Looking down on the field below, he noticed there was no fighting to be seen. Many of the opposing soldiers looked confused, and the creatures were nowhere in sight. "It looks like he freed more than just the people in the gems," he said. Placing an arm around Kaiya, he said, "Come on. Let's find the king and be done with this place."

She nodded slowly, allowing him to help her as she stood. Moving toward the door, she looked back, hoping to see River's face once more, but he was not there.

Chapter 25

Isandra stood back-to-back with King Rykon, the two of them surrounded by enemy soldiers. They held their swords high, the runes shining brightly through a thick coating of partially dried blood. No matter how hard they fought, they could not subdue enough of Ulda's undead minions to make any difference in the fighting. They had paused for only seconds at a time, their muscles aching from overuse and fatigue.

A low rumble cut through the noise of battle, and Isandra's eyes wandered away from her opponents to the spire where she had left her father and his companions. It appeared to be vibrating, chunks of rock dropping from its sides. "The tower is collapsing!" she shouted to the king.

Rykon looked away, and many of the enemy soldiers did as well. After a tense moment, the tower ceased its shaking, bright lights bursting from its narrow windows. Many of the soldiers dropped to their knees, grasping at their helmets as if they'd suffered severe blows to the head. But neither Isandra nor Rykon was to blame.

"What's happening?" Isandra asked.

Rykon appeared puzzled, but said, "They're in pain. Something has happened inside the tower."

Isandra closed her eyes. "My father was successful," she said. Opening her eyes, she looked out across the battlefield. Where once stood legions of wolfmen and tigers were now only elves—the ones Ulda had defiled to craft his twisted minions. She pointed out into the distance, where a single sorcerer fell from the sky, his wyvern nowhere to be seen.

Rykon swung around to look upon the tower, and a smile graced his visage. Two figures emerged, striding with ease toward him. Too small to be River or Telorithan, he was certain it was Mel and Kaiya who approached.

The king raised his sword, crying out to his soldiers, "The battle is won!" A great cry of triumph echoed throughout the field, some of Ulda's former slaves joining in as well. Those who were aware of their situation had been given no choice in their actions, and they were glad to be free of their former master's grasp. Others appeared confused, not knowing what had been happening over the past several months, or even years. They would need time to heal and recover their memories.

Mel waved a hand to the king, his other hand still resting on Kaiya's shoulder. The pair moved closer, their faces more somber than Rykon had expected.

"You bring grave news," the king said.

Kaiya looked at the ground. "River is gone," she said.

Mel added, "Telorithan is gone too. It was the only way." After a moment, he said, "When I added my magic to his at the end, I didn't expect it to happen." His words were full of regret. If he hadn't joined his powers with River and Kaiya to free the bound souls, perhaps River would still be alive.

Without lifting her head, Kaiya said, "I knew it would happen. This feat would have been impossible without River's sacrifice. No single elemental has the power to free a bound soul, and it required his entire being to break Ulda's hold over these people." She looked around, taking in the thousands of lives that were now safe.

Rykon bowed his head in reverence, remembering his fallen friend.

Isandra could not contain her emotions, and the tears streamed down her face. Removing her helmet, she wiped her eyes with the back of her hand and looked up at the tower. "My father knew the cost," she said. "It was a sacrifice he was most willing to make. I only regret the pain this will cause my mother."

Kaiya looked up at Isandra, her eyes full of tears. "I will return to the Vale with you and speak with her."

Isandra nodded. Lenora considered Kaiya a dear friend, and she would take comfort in the dwarf's presence in her time of grief.

"We will honor his memory in Na'zora as well," the king said. "And Telorithan as well. He must not be forgotten in this."

Mel nodded his agreement. Looking out among Ulda's former slaves, he asked, "What do we do about them?"

Rykon replied, "I will leave soldiers to assist the people of Ral'nassa. There is much work ahead of us, but Na'zora will see it done."

Mel turned his attention to the sea. "It looks like the elementals are still holding the bridge for us. Maybe we should get going before they change their minds."

Isandra looked out over the blue and said, "My father will see us home safely."

* * * * *

Lenora sat beneath the weeping willow, staring out over the river. Alyra lay at her side, her head nestled in her mother's lap. The pounding of the waterfall echoed in the girl's ears as she dozed beneath the cloudless sky.

Lenora sat idly twirling a finger in her daughter's dark hair, her eyes ever staring at the water. As she watched, the colorless river slowly changed to deep blue.

Sitting forward in her seat, she disturbed Alyra, who bolted upright. "What is it, Mother?" she asked.

Lenora pointed to the sparkling blue water. "The river," she said, her voice barely more than a whisper.

Alyra looked at the water and smiled. "He did it!" she shouted, throwing her arms around her mother.

Grasping her daughter tightly, Lenora's eyes glistened with joy. If Ulda was defeated, her life mate would be returning home. But a feeling of dread crept over her, her mind not allowing her to ignore the truth. She knew what was required of him, and she knew what Ulda's defeat had cost her.

Turning to face the water, she gripped her daughter's hand. How would she tell the child her father would not be coming home? As she contemplated the words to use, a blue mist formed above the river, gliding gently across the shining surface. Growing smaller on its approach, Lenora watched it move closer and closer. Stretching out her hands, she cupped the mist and brought it closer to her face. Warmth and comfort swept over her, tears spilling from her eyes. A joyous smile spread across her lips as the light moved away, disappearing into the depths of the Blue River. Her life mate had indeed come home.

Epilogue

Lenora waded into the river, as she did every morning. Here within the depths, her life mate patiently awaited her. Her blue gown danced softly on the surface of the cool water as she waded toward the base of the waterfall.

Silently she stood, waiting for her love to appear. Peering deep into the water, she beheld a familiar blue light swirling just beneath the surface. A sense of peace rushed over her, and she lay back, resting her head upon the water's surface. Wrapping herself in the presence of her life mate, she surrendered herself to the ever-changing current. Sleep overcame her, and she closed her eyes to the world.

When she awoke, she found herself lying on the riverbank. Sitting up, she stretched her arms and turned her gaze to the sunlight glinting off the water's surface. A warm breeze caressed her cheek, and her heart filled with hope. As she looked out over the water, she could feel River's presence, his sapphire blue eyes still watching over her.

Lifting herself to her feet, she climbed up the bank to her village. As she walked, she realized she was not alone. A second heart was beating within her. Placing her hands on her midsection, she turned back to the river and smiled.

About the Author

Lana Axe lives in the Missouri countryside surrounded by dogs, cats, birds, and reptiles. She spends most of her free time daydreaming about elves, magic, and faraway lands.

For more information, please visit: lana-axe.com.